JACKIE GOES
TO DIXIE

OTHER BOOKS BY MICHAEL B. DRUXMAN

FICTION

Murder in Babylon

Dracula Meets Jack the Ripper & Other Revisionist Histories

Once Upon A Time In Hollywood: From the Secret Files of Harry Pennypacker

Shadow Watcher

Nobody Drowns In Mineral Lake

NON-FICTION

Hollywood Snapshots: The Forgotten Interviews

Miss Dinah Shore

Life, Liberty & The Pursuit of Hollywood

My Forty-Five Years In Hollywood And How I Escaped Alive

Family Secret (with Warren Hull)

The Art of Storytelling

The Musical: From Broadway To Hollywood

One Good Film Deserves Another

Charlton Heston

Merv

Make It Again, Sam

Basil Rathbone: His Life and His Films

Paul Muni: His Life And His Films

OTHER STAGE PLAYS

Hail on the Chief!

Putz

The Summer Folk

STAGE PLAYS (THE HOLLYWOOD LEGENDS)

Ava & Her Guys

The Last Monsters

Robinson & Raft

Lana & Johnny Were Lovers

Sexy Rexy

B Movie

Clara Bow

Chevalier

Flynn

Gable

Jolson

Lombard

Nelson and Jeanette

Rathbone

Tracy

Orson Welles

SCREENPLAYS

The Amusement

Barry & The Bimbo

Black Watch / The Cavern

Charla

Cheyenne Warrior

Cheyenne Warrior II / Hawk

Ghoul City

Matricide

Ride Along

Sarah Golden Hair

The Summer Folk

Uncle Louie

JACKIE GOES TO DIXIE

A NOVEL

by

Michael B. Druxman

BearManor Media

2017

Jackie Goes to Dixie

© 2017 Michael B. Druxman

Jackie Goes to Dixie is a work of fiction. Any similarity to persons living or dead is purely coincidental.

For information, address:

BearManor Media
P. O. Box 71426
Albany, GA 31708

bearmanormedia.com

Typesetting and layout by John Teehan

Published in the USA by BearManor Media

ISBN—978-1-62933-168-3

IN MEMORY OF

Jack Carter
Jackie Vernon
Stanley Myron Handelman
and
Don Rickles

CHAPTER ONE

Did I ever tell you about the time I almost got lynched? It happened back in the mid-1970s in a place called Buford, Arkansas. That's way up in the Ozark Mountains.

You're probably wondering what Dave Arthur, a fifty-year-old Jewish piano player and movie buff from New York, was doing in hillbilly country.

I was working. My boss, Jackie Moss, also a fifty-year-old Jew from New York, had a gig there.

Actually, he's the one that the folks in Buford really wanted to lynch. They were just taking me along for the ride.

If you're old enough, you'll remember Jackie Moss. He was one of America's top stand-up comics.

Excuse me. Jackie hated the word "comic." He was a "comedian."

Back in the day, there was Don Rickles, Jack Carter, Buddy Hackett and Jackie Moss. They headlined every major nightclub in the country. They appeared regularly on every television variety and talk show. Audiences loved them. They were legends in their own time.

Now, you're probably wondering why the hell, if Jackie Moss was such a legend in his own time, he was working in a *farkakte (his term)* place like Buford.

The truth is that that's the only job he could get by then, and he got that one strictly by accident.

I guess I should start at the beginning.

Jackie and I go way back. We went to school together; joined the army together. We were both stationed in Japan; worked the USO shows that entertained our troops that were stationed there. He told the jokes. I played the piano and, after we were both discharged, he asked me to accompany him as his pianist/musical director when he played the Greenwich Village clubs and Catskill resorts, which led to his being asked to appear on television shows like *Ed Sullivan* and *Milton Berle*.

After that, his career took off...and I went with him as his accompanist, musical director and road manager. He did major nightclubs. He did movies, usually playing the short, pudgy, slightly balding best friend of the romantic lead. And, he even got his own television series, a sitcom, *The Jackie Moss Show*, which was cancelled after the first thirteen episodes. The network blamed the show's poor ratings on the fact that Jackie didn't exude a warmth that would make viewers want to invite him into their homes every week, whereas Jackie was convinced that the series was sabotaged from the start. "A bunch of no talent schmucks produced it," he'd say, "and they'd never listen to my input."

Jackie and I both got married. After twenty years, Doris and I were still going strong, but Jackie's marriage to Barbara collapsed three years after his son, Jason, was born. He just couldn't resist the temptation of all those "star fuckers" he'd meet when we were on the road and, finally, Barb, a dancer and former Rockette, had had enough. She took Jason, filed for divorce and moved back to her hometown of Cincinnati, Ohio.

He may have been a lousy husband, but Jackie sure missed his son. He'd send presents every week, call him every Sunday, and when he had some time off, he'd fly into Cincinnati from his home in Los Angeles for a visit. There was nothing he wouldn't do for Jason.

Jackie was never "easy." Actually, I don't think that any comics – excuse me, *comedians* – are "easy." They're paranoid. They all seem to have a deep-seated anger inside them, probably stemming from feelings of being unloved during their childhoods. I'm no psychiatrist, so I'm not going to delve into that psychology any further, except to say that, on stage, Jackie was funniest when he was angriest.

I remember a night in Vegas. Jackie was headlining at the Sahara. Just before he went on stage, he was leaning against the proscenium arch and he snagged the shoulder of his tux on a protruding nail. He was pissed when he walked out on stage, but he delivered the funniest sixty minutes of his career. His ranting resulted in non-stop laughter from the audience.

Anger, of course, has its downside. In addition to the break-up of his marriage, Jackie was not happy with his career. Yes, he was considered one of the top funnymen in the country, but when it came to television or the movies, he was, essentially, a "second banana." He didn't want to be the hero's comedy sidekick. He wanted to star in his own movies, like Jerry Lewis and Bob Hope.

The frustration ate at him. He grumbled. He snapped at people, and they shied away from him. He snapped at me, and I told him to go fuck himself.

I don't think he fucked himself, but he did respect the fact that I stood up to him. He knew that I was his friend.

But, his surliness started affecting his work. Sometimes audiences weren't sure if he was kidding…or truly angry. Bookings began to taper off.

But, Jackie's *real* problem began about two years before the Buford occurrence.

Do you remember the country/western singer, Jake Moss? He was a young guy, probably in his early twenties, sort of a cross between Elvis Presley and Johnny Cash. He was quite hot during most of the 1970s. Audiences loved him, particularly women.

Jackie's dilemma was that, because of the similarities of their names (i.e. Jackie Moss/Jake Moss), people, including club managers, were getting them mixed up and some gigs that should have gone to Jackie went to this new usurper.

Compounding the situation was the fact that, in the 1970s, Jackie's brash approach to comedy was going out of style. Audiences, especially the younger ones, were gravitating toward the low-key comedians, like Bill Cosby, Stanley Myron Handelman and Rip Taylor, or, as Jackie called them, "the cutesy comics." Legendary comedians, like Jackie Moss, were beginning to feel like dinosaurs.

Everything pretty much came to a head one night in Vegas. Jackie's last two dates there hadn't gone well. He'd played to less than full houses. Hell, those big rooms weren't even half filled, so now he was playing the lounge at the Jackpot, a small hotel located a block off the Strip.

And, Jake Moss was headlining at the Tropicana.

Jackie wasn't happy about that.

Still, Jackie's first show had almost a full house. I was at the piano, backed by a drummer and a guy playing bass.

Jackie strolled out on stage, not in the greatest mood since he'd just dropped a grand at the crap table. After my intro music and the applause stopped, he began his act.

"I used to play the Strip," he said. "I opened for Sinatra at the Sands…I headlined at the Sahara…the Riviera….And now, my manager's got me playing the lounge at this *farkakte* joint…. What's next for me? The coffee shop at the Greyhound depot?"

The audience chuckled, but not Ray Crystal. He was Jackie's personal manager, and that dapper dresser was sitting alone at a table in the back of the room with a deadpan expression on his face. You really couldn't blame Ray for *not* laughing. At fifty-five and after thirty years in the business, he'd heard Jackie…and a few other comedians…tell jokes like these before. He was immune.

"What is this?" Jackie continued to the audience. "*The Night of the Living Dead?* …These are the jokes, folks. They don't get any better."

A nervous titter spread through the audience.

"Don't I got a right to be angry?" Jackie said. "I've been Jackie Moss for twenty years. Then, two years ago, that hillbilly singer, who's stinking up the Tropicana, comes along… calls himself *Jake* Moss…and steals my audience.….I'll bet that half the dumb schmucks watchin' him right now thought they were goin' to see me."

There were a few more chuckles from the audience. I began to wonder if they were starting to laugh *at* Jackie, rather than *with* him.

"And, this Jake Moss character isn't even a relative," Jackie said. "I can't even go to him to borrow money."

I caught Crystal cracking a smile at that line. Then, I spotted Vic Newland, the forty-year-old, balding manager of the Jackpot. He was standing at the lounge entry, motioning Crystal to join him. Ray got up and headed in his direction.

"You know what makes a good country-western singer?" Jackie continued. "Inbreeding!"

There was another mild laugh from the audience, as Crystal and Newland headed out into the casino area.

Jackie noticed a young couple in their twenties, sitting at a front table. "You're a nice looking couple," he said. "Newlyweds?"

The couple nodded.

Jackie looked at the groom. "Where'd you pick her up at? The bar?"

The couple laughed, somewhat embarrassed.

"Fella," Jackie continued, "didn't your dad ever tell you? You just give these gals a couple hundred bucks. You don't have to marry them."

The couple wasn't sure whether they should laugh or not, and neither was the audience. There was dead silence. In fact, it was pretty quiet for the rest of the act.

"What's the matter with them?" Jackie grumbled, as we retreated toward his dressing room. "Don't they know funny stuff when they hear it?"

"It was just a dead house," I said.

"Jack the Ripper couldn't make them any deader."

"Next show, they'll laugh." Placating him was another of my duties.

"Next show, they're liable to attack."

Mindy, a scantily clad blonde show girl, walked by us, heading for the stage. "Hi, Jack," she said.

Jackie forced a smile. "Hi, honey."

When we got to Jackie's dressing room, Ray Crystal was sitting on the sofa waiting for us. He had a dour expression on his face.

He didn't say anything. Neither did Jackie, who doffed his jacket and poured himself a drink. I knew what was coming, so I retreated into the bathroom to "freshen up." The door was shut, but I could hear everything.

"Okay," Jackie said, finally, "so I got angry out there."

"Rabid is more like it," Crystal said.

"Stop, already."

"Angry," Crystal continued, "you're funny…. Tonight, you were mean, bitter, insulting, and, Jack, it's getting worse."

"Rickles does the same thing and the schmucks love it."

"They love it because they know that Don doesn't mean it," Crystal said. "Tonight, I wasn't sure if I was watching Jackie Moss or Joseph Mengele out there."

"I'll tone it down," Jackie muttered.

"You'd better," Crystal said. "If you do another show like that, Newland's canceling the rest of your gig."

"He said that?"

"Twenty minutes ago."

"Bullshit!" Jackie said. "How else is he going to collect on my markers?"

"Vegas always collects, even if they have to take your first born son."

"Ha!" Jackie said. "Tell them they're out of luck there. The wife got the kid...and everything else in the settlement."

I could hear him pour himself another drink. Then, after a moment, he said, "Tell Newland I'll try to be good."

"That's all he expects, Jack," Crystal said. "Don't worry. Things will get better."

"Yeah," Jackie said.

Crystal departed, and then I came out of the bathroom.

"Did you hear that?" Jackie asked.

I nodded.

"That son-of-a-bitch Newland is threatening to cancel my gig."

He was beginning to fume. I knew better that to try deal with him when he was in that mode. The only word that came to my mind was "Oy!.."

The house for the second show was half full. Crystal was at his table in the back of the room. Newland was watching from the lounge entrance.

I walked onto the stage and over to the piano, then cued the other musicians. We began to play "Lullaby of Broadway," Jackie's introduction music. "Ladies and gentlemen," I announced into the mike on the piano, "Mr. Jackie Moss!."

The audience applauded. Jackie strolled onto the stage wearing a killer smile that reminded me of Burt Lancaster in *Vera Cruz*, a Western he'd made with Gary Cooper. Every time that Burt had smiled that way in the movie, somebody was about to get shot.

The applause died down. Jackie didn't say a word. He just surveyed the audience until he spotted Newland. "Hey, Vic!" he waved to the hotel manager.

Newland gave him a wary nod.

"That's Vic Newland over there," Jackie said to the audience. "He's the manager of this toilet."

Some of the audience turned to look in Newland's direction.

"He's the guy with the bald head and the little dick," Jackie continued. "Or, is it the little head and the bald dick? I can't remember."

The audience seemed confused, as Newland stomped out of the room. Crystal buried his head in his hands, and I sat at the piano with my mouth agape.

Jackie looked over at me and shrugged. "Guess I did it again," he said.

We were on the last plane back to Los Angeles that night. Jackie and I sat in first class, but Ray Crystal had traded his first class ticket with some fellow sitting in coach.

"I don't get it," Jackie mumbled. "What's he doing back there?"

"He doesn't want to talk to you," I said.

"He's my manager. How can he not talk to me?"

"He's afraid he might get violent."

Jackie took another swallow of his scotch. "I don't get it," he said. "So, I blew the gig. I didn't want to play that dump anyhow."

"Jack," I said, "you don't have any gigs left. After that one-nighter next week in Arkansas, you've got a free calendar."

"Arkansas! I'd rather play the coffee shop at the Greyhound bus depot."

He was shouting now, and other passengers, some of whom were trying to snooze on the short flight, were taking notice.

"The bus depot won't pay you twenty-five grand for a one night gig," I whispered.

He didn't have an answer for that one. He just turned and looked out the window at the night sky.

"Jack," I said, "can I be frank with you?

"Frank…Joe…Irving…. Be whoever you want," he said.

"You know, you've never been easy, but when you were with Barbara, you were more 'docile."

"Docile!?! You're saying I was a poodle?"

"You were easier to get along with."

"And, what am I now? A Jewish Rottweiler?"

"Have you ever thought of going to a psychiatrist? It might help…with the anger."

"Hey, I'm an angry man," he said, his voice rising again. "My father was an angry man. It's in the genes."

I decided to back off. "Okay," I said, "it was just a suggestion."

"Actually, I've got a psychiatrist," Jack said. "He won't talk to me either."

I couldn't help chuckling at that last line. Jackie picked up on that and ran with it. "Right now," he said, "you're the only one in my life that'll talk to me…except my mother. And, she only talks to me because I bring her a check every week and eat her Gefilte fish."

We were standing by the carousel at LAX baggage claim, waiting for our luggage to come sliding down the chute, when Crystal, stone-faced, approached us. "Breaking your silence?" Jackie said with a smirk.

"Don't say a word," Crystal snapped. "If I hear one word…one syllable…emerge from your mouth before you return from Arkansas, I will immediately terminate our contract. Do you understand the English that I am speaking to you, or must I translate what I just said into another language?"

Jackie knew that Ray meant business. He nodded and placed his hand over his mouth.

"First," Crystal continued, "you'll be happy to learn that Vic Newland has agreed to tear up your markers, *providing* that we agree not to press for payment on the ten days of your contract that he cancelled."

Jackie started to object.

"Not one syllable!"

Jackie shut up.

"Second, I will messenger over the tickets and itinerary for the Arkansas engagement…and if I hear one negative word… one negative syllable…about your behavior there, our shredded agreement will be waiting at your home when you get back.

"So, do you understand? Just nod."

Jackie desperately wanted to say something, but he just nodded.

"Fine," Crystal said, and then he headed for the exit.

"Think he means it?" Jackie asked, as he watched his manager depart.

"I think he means it," I said.

We grabbed our suitcases off the carousel, and then walked outside to grab a taxi. "Buford, Arkansas," Jackie moaned. "That's hillbilly heaven."

"Obviously you've got fans there," I said.

CHAPTER TWO

The flight to Little Rock was uneventful. I slept most of the way, so I didn't have to listen to Jackie's grumbling.

Edward Webster, a tall, lanky black man in his fifties, wearing a chauffeur's uniform that didn't quite fit, met us at the airport. He had graying temples, a mustache, and spoke in a subservient manner, yet I had the feeling that he was a lot smarter than he wanted anybody to know.

As he loaded our luggage into the trunk of the Cadillac limousine, he told us that he had been born in Buford, but had left when he was a young man to work in a factory "up North." He'd retuned home about five years ago to care for his ailing grandfather, who had since passed.

The drive up into the Ozarks was certainly scenic. The two-lane, blacktopped road wound its way through forests, over rivers and streams; past unusual rock formations, as well as an occasional abandoned, rusted car or truck. There were few other vehicles on the road; if you didn't count the half dozen riders on horseback or mule that we passed.

Jackie and I were in the back seat of the limo, separated from the front by a glass partition. About two hours into the trip, Jackie leaned over to me and whispered, "He keeps staring at us."

"Who?" I asked.

"The driver. He hasn't taken his eyes off us since we left the airport."

I glanced up and Edward was, indeed, checking us out through his rearview mirror. "Maybe he's never seen a celebrity before," I said.

"It's not that kind of look," Jackie said. "He reached over and slid back the glass partition. "How soon 'til we get there?" he asked Edward.

"'Bout another hour, sir."

"We're really going to Hell and gone," Jackie muttered.

"Yeah, Buford's kinda off the beaten track, sir," Edward said. "But, we got all the modern conveniences."

"So, what's its 'horse'?"

"No horses, sir," Edward said. "Us folks all drive cars."

"No," Jackie said, "I meant…what industry supports the town? Farming?"

"Most folks here abouts work at The Factory."

"What kind of factory?"

"Toilet seats," Edward said. "The finest toilet seats in the South come from Buford."

Jackie chuckled. "That's good," he said. "I can use that."

"They also make some kind of doo-hickey for the Navy."

"Doo-hickey?" Jackie asked.

"It's this little thing they put in their missiles," Edward said. "A doo-hickey."

"Toilet seats and doo-hickeys," Jackie mused. "That's quite a combination." He pondered a moment, and then said, "The reason I'm asking you, Edward, is because I always put some local color into my act. Audiences dig it."

"We got plenty of color here, sir," Edward said. "Now, me, I play the guitar. Sing a little…."

"Good to know," Jackie said, closing the partition; sitting back into his seat.

Jackie had to use the john, so Edward stopped at a service station, an old wood structure at the side of the road with ancient gas pumps, a vintage Coke machine and an outhouse out back. The attendant, an elderly black man, dozed in his rocking chair by the front door.

While Jackie was using the "facilities," Edward and I stood in the shade, drinking Cokes.

"Mr. Moss sure don't look like his pictures," Edward said.

"Maybe it's an old picture," I said with a shrug.

Jackie emerged from the outhouse, and he didn't look happy. "Thought you said that Buford had all the modern conveniences," he said to Edward.

"We ain't in Buford yet," Edward replied.

"They got plenty of reading material in that shit hole, but no toilet paper."

"That ain't reading material," Edward said.

"Oh!" Getting Edward's meaning and stuck for a comeback line, Jackie walked over to for the Coke machine. "I could use something cold," he said.

Sipping his soft drink, Jackie joined us in the shade. "So, tell me, Edward," he said, "what's Buford's mayor like?"

"We don't got no mayor?"

"Then, who runs the town?"

"The Colonel," Edward said. "He's the boss. He's some kinda engineer. Invented the doo-hickey."

"Interesting," Jackie said.

"The General, he used to run it," Edward continued, "but he's retired now."

"So, you got a Marine base in Buford?"

Edward chuckled. "No, you don't understand," he said. "The Colonel and the General ain't really military. They just call themselves by them names. Sort of a holdover from the Civil War."

Jackie looked at me. "Do you understand this?" he asked.

I just shrugged.

"See," Edward continued, "they're all one family. The Dawsons."

"The Dawsons?"

"That's right," Edward said. "There's the General and his sons, the Colonel…an' the Major. He kinda runs things when the Colonel's not around."

"Makes sense," Jackie said, trying not to laugh.

"Then, there's the Major's boy, the Corporal," Edward said. "He don't do much of anything."

"The General fought in the Civil War?" Jackie asked.

"His granddaddy did," Edward said. "He's the reason you're here. Tonight's his ninetieth birthday party."

"No offense," Edward," Jackie said, "but do they still keep slaves here to pick the cotton?"

Edward chuckled again. "We don't have no cotton in Buford, sir," he said. "And, as far as the rest of it, let's just say that it's to our advantage to call ourselves 'Negroes' 'stead of 'Blacks'. 'Fact, if you and Mr. Arthur feel more comfortable referring to us as 'schwartzas,' that's okay, too…. You get my meaning?"

"You're a pretty smart fella, Edward," Jackie said.

"Thank you, sir."

For the rest of the drive through the mountains, Jackie and I sat in the back seat of the limo, partition up, while he made notes for his act on the back of an envelope. "This is some good stuff," he said, chuckling at his own cleverness. "Am I going to be hot tonight!"

The glint in Jackie's eye bothered me. It was the same sort of glint he had when he walked out onto the stage for that last show at the Jackpot.

"You can improvise a little 'Dixie," can't you?" he asked.

"Jack," I said, "I'd be careful. This isn't a Vegas audience."

"My last Vegas audience sat there with their arms folded and frowns painted on their faces," he said. "What's this one going to do? Lynch me?"

If only we knew then….

B uford was a throwback to a long bygone era.
Virtually all of the buildings, one or two story wood-frame and old brick structures, were built during the nineteenth or first part of the twentieth centuries. Most of the sidewalks were wood, but the street itself was blacktopped. The vehicles we saw were also older cars and pick-up trucks.

There was a general store, some saloons, a barber/beauty shop, a real estate office and a few other staple businesses. Indeed, about the only store that seemed to recognize any form of modern technology was one that sold various appliances. An antiquated model refrigerator and a color television set, with a feeble picture quality, were in the display window.

There were a few people on the street. They were dressed in casual work clothes, a few years out of fashion. Each one turned and tried to get a look inside the limo as we passed by. "Is that him?" I heard a greatly overweight woman in a print dress say to her skinny companion.

"Must be," the other woman said.

Edward pointed to a large, two-story building, set back on a hill above the town. It had a tall smokestack protruding from its roof, was surrounded by a chain-link security fence and, as we would learn later, was patrolled by armed uniformed guards. "That's The Factory," he said. "That's where they make the toilet seats and doo-hickeys."

Jackie turned to me, a bit bemused. "You're right," he said. "It ain't Vegas…. It ain't even Walla Walla, Washington."

Edward stopped the Cadillac in front of another two-story, wood-frame building which looked like it dated back at least sixty or seventy years. A marquee over the entrance awning announced "GRAND HOTEL," while a paper banner below that proclaimed, "WELCOME J. MOSS."

A metal fire escape adorned the front of the structure, but there seemed to be few, if any, other modern improvements or major efforts to change the historic façade.

I looked at Jackie as he stepped out of the car. His expression reminded me of Judy Garland's when she'd first found herself in the Land of Oz. "What's this?" he asked.

"Your hotel," Edward said.

Jackie shook his head. "This isn't my hotel," he said.

"It's the only hotel in town."

"You don't have a Hilton? A Holiday Inn? How about a Motel 6?"

"We don't get many visitors here in Buford," Edward said.

A few citizens had gathered and were giving Jackie, who was experiencing a rare loss of words, the once over.

"You go inside, sir," Edward continued. "I'll get your luggage."

Jackie's face started to redden. "You expect me to go inside this...."

"Do it, Jack," I whispered, taking hold of his arm. "Don't make a scene."

He knew I was right. He shut up, and then headed toward the hotel entrance. Glancing up at the banner that read, "WELCOME J. MOSS," he muttered, "They couldn't even spell out my name?"

In the crowd of onlookers, I heard the overweight woman ask, "Is that him?" and her skinny friend reply, "Must be.."

Maintaining the décor of its grand beginnings, the lobby of the Grand Hotel was decorated in red velvets and yellow brass fittings. There were several sofas, a chandelier, an oak registration desk and a curved staircase to the second floor.

There was only one other person in the lobby when Jackie and I stepped inside; a distinguished, bearded gent in his forties, dressed in a dark, fashionable suit. He was sitting near the large plate glass window, reading a hardbound book. I would later learn that his name was Paul Babin.

Jackie glanced around the room and announced, "It looks like a whorehouse."

"It is."

We turned to see a gorgeous brunette enter from a door behind the registration desk. She was about forty, attired in a bright summer dress and she didn't seem to belong in this rural setting any more than Jackie and I did.

"Or, at least, it was back in my great grandmother's day," she said, walking toward us, extending her hand. "I'm Angie Benedict. Welcome to Buford, Mr....." Suddenly, she seemed to recognize Jackie, and she looked surprised. "Mr. Moss, what are you doing here?"

"I'm entertaining at some old guy's birthday party," Jackie said, turning on the charm.

"The General's party?" she said, her surprise shifting into shock. "You?"

"Hey," Jackie said, a bit taken aback, "I'm not going to jump out of a cake naked."

"Wait a minute," she said, trying to collect her thoughts, and then Edward entered with our luggage. They caught each other's eye. "Why don't you go over and sign the registration book," she said to us.

"Take care of it," Jackie said to me.

Okay, from this point forward, I will, from time to time, be relating some moments during our visit to Buford that I did not personally witness. However, after the fact, Jackie and/or others recounted them to me with remarkable detail.

As I was signing the guest book, I could hear Edward and Miss Benedict whispering. "There's been a mistake," she said.

Edward nodded. "I know," he said. "I guess the Corporal did it again."

"Somebody's got to tell them."

"Not me," Edward said.

Suddenly I realized what they were talking about, and I knew that the shit was about to hit the fan.

While this was going on, Jackie wandered about the lobby and struck up a conversation with Paul Babin, who spoke with a mid-Central European accent. "Hello," he said to Jackie.

"Hiya,"

"I've seen you in motion picture films, haven't I?" Babin said.

"I hope so," Jackie said. "You sound European?"

"Prague."

"Never played there."

Babin chuckled.

"They paid me to come to this place," Jackie said. "What's your excuse?"

"I'm a buyer."

"You came all the way from Prague to buy toilet seats?"

Babin smiled. "Industrial equipment," he said.

"Oh," Jackie said, "doo-hickeys."

"I beg your pardon?"

"Never mind." Jackie said. "Nice talkin' to you." His eye on Miss Benedict, he headed back in my direction. "She's a looker," he whispered to me.

"Something's not right here, Jack," I said.

"You're telling me?" He didn't get my meaning.

"Mr. Moss," Angie Benedict said, walking over to us, "Are you sure you've been hired to play the General's party?"

"Paid for in advance," Jackie replied. "Why?"

"Well," she said, "I don't want to upset you…."

"I've seen the town," Jackie interjected. "How much more upset can I be?

She didn't answer; just threw a glance at Edward, who was standing a few steps behind her.

"What?" Jackie said.

"You're *Jackie* Moss, the comedian, right?" she said.

"Yes…"

"We were told," she said, "that they had booked *Jake* Moss, the singer."

I watched Jackie, waiting for him to explode.

"I don't know how this could have happened," she continued. "Well, actually I do know…"

Suddenly, Jackie started to laugh. "Son-of-a-bitch!" he said.

"Jack…?" I said

He continued to laugh. "I finally did it," he said.

"Did what?" Angie Benedict asked. "I don't understand."

She looked at Edward, who looked like he was as confused as I was.

"What goes around, comes around, honey," Jackie said. "That inbred bastard has been knocking me out of gigs for years. And now, I've got one of his."

"Jack," I said, trying to curtail his continuing guffaws.

"Mr. Moss," Angie Benedict said, "you don't seem to understand. The people here are expecting to see *Jake* Moss. I don't think…."

"And, they got me," Jackie interrupted. "I know."

"They're not really your kind of audience," she said.

"She's right, Jack," I said.

Jackie stopped laughing. "Well. That's tough shit, isn't it?" he snapped. "Can we have the key to our rooms? I'd like to freshen up before the show."

Angie Benedict hesitated for a long moment, and then she handed us our keys. "Upstairs," she said. "First two doors on the right. Edward will bring up your bags."

"Thanks," Jackie said. Then, he looked at me. "Coming," he asked.

I wasn't about to make another scene in the lobby in front of strangers, so I followed him upstairs.

After we were out of sight, Edward approached Angie Benedict. "You told them," he said. "Now, who's gonna tell the Colonel?"

Still sitting by the window, Paul Babin closed his book. "Tonight should be a very interesting evening," he said.

CHAPTER THREE

Before Angie Benedict called, the Colonel and the Major were in a heated discussion in the Colonel's upstairs office at The Factory.

Frank Dawson (aka: the Colonel) was in his mid-fifties, tall and a bit beefy; with his snappy manner of talking, he could probably have passed as a redneck version of actor Broderick Crawford in his younger days.

And for those of you who don't remember Broderick Crawford, take a look at *All the King's Men* or *Born Yesterday* the next time they play on TCM.

On the other hand, William (aka: the Major), his younger brother by five years, was the complete opposite; a handsome, strapping fellow who, as I would soon learn, liked the ladies almost as much as he resented his brother.

There was also another person in the room, if not in body, then in presence. Hanging on the wall was a portrait of James Dawson (aka: the General), dressed in a World War One Army officer's uniform. It was one of those creepy portraits where the eyes followed you everywhere.

"I don't care what he's offering," the Colonel said to his brother, lighting another cigarette, "we're not interested."

"He's offering five million, Frank," the Major said, "and that's just for starters."

"Five million. Twenty million.... We got one customer, William. That's the United States Government."

"Yeah, but...."

The Colonel cut him off. "The quickest way to get the military to come in here," he said, "and set up shop is for us to start talkin' to other people. You want a Marine guard stationed outside our factory?"

"No...."

"Then, drop it!"

And, that's when the phone rang.

The Colonel picked up the receiver. "This is the Colonel," he growled.

The voice on the other end of the line was hesitant. "Frank...?"

"Angie!" the Colonel said, brightening his tone. "I hear you got a new dress for the party tonight. Pretty one."

"How'd you know that?" Angie Benedict asked.

"I know everything that goes on in Buford, honey. Don't you know that yet?"

"Well, do you know Jackie Moss?"

The Colonel looked at his brother. "Jackie Moss, do we know him?"

"He's some Jew comedian," the Major said. "We've seen him on the TV."

'Oh, him," the Colonel said, then into the phone. "Yeah. What about him?"

"He's entertaining at the party tonight."

"He's *what*!?!"

"He's entertaining at the party tonight," Angie Benedict repeated.

"What about the singer?"

"I don't know," Angie Benedict said. "I guess somebody screwed up."

The Colonel glowered at his brother, then bid his caller "goodbye" and hung up.

"What?" the Major asked.

"Who did you hire to entertain at our Daddy's party tonight?"

"Jake Moss, the singer," the Major said. "I gave Junior all the information and then told him to…." He blanched. "Oh, shit!" he said.

"Yeah," said the Colonel, "Oh shit!"

The ground floor of The Factory was like a huge warehouse. Against one wall was a locked chain-linked gated area, sealing off a room, marked "Authorized Personnel Only." A sign below that one read, "If you're not authorized, GO AWAY,"

In the center of the large space, assembly-line workers kept busy, making the company's toilet sets, while at the end of that line, against another wall, was the supervisor's desk, manned by a lanky, pimple-faced young man in his mid-twenties, intent on watching a Mighty Mouse cartoon on his desktop television screen.

This was the Major's son, Billy, Jr. (aka: The Corporal), known throughout Buford as being two cans short of a six-pack.

Every pair of eyes on the assembly line remained glued to the angry Colonel and the equally angry Major as they entered the workplace and strode toward the Corporal's desk. They knew there was going to be a "show," and they didn't want to miss it. Indeed, the only person not aware of the brothers was the Corporal, still involved in his cartoon…until the screen went black after the Colonel reached over and pulled the plug on the television set.

"Damn it, Uncle Frank," the Corporal said, "What'd you do that for?"

His father corrected him. "At work, it's 'Colonel, sir'," he said.

"Yeah, Daddy," the Corporal said, pointing to the television screen, "but that was Mighty Mouse."

On the assembly line, one of the workers began humming the Mighty Mouse theme: "Here he comes to save the day…"

"I'll *mighty mouse* you," the Major said to his son, throwing a cold glance at the assembly line.

The worker shut up.

"And, it's 'Major,' Corporal," he continued. "Or, do we bust you back down to Private?"

"You bust me again, and I'll quit."

"Don't tempt me," the Major said.

The Colonel stepped between father and son. "Corporal…Billy…," he said, "your father says that he had you hire the talent for Grandpa's party tonight."

"Yeah…" the Corporal said.

"Who'd you hire?"

"The singer that Grandpa likes. The one Daddy told me to."

"I didn't…."

The Colonel cut off his brother. "What was his name?" he said.

"Moss," the Corporal said. "Jakie Moss."

The two older men glowered at him.

"What?" the Corporal said.

"It's *Jake*, you idiot!" the Major screamed. "Not *Jakie*! And, not *Jackie*!"

"What's the difference?" the Corporal asked.

The Major, suddenly, picked up the television from his son's desk and smashed it down onto the ground. "That's the difference," he said.

The Corporal backed away, as his father stared at him with a look that could kill. Behind them, the assembly line workers sniggered, as they pretended to do their work.

The Colonel turned to his brother. "Bill, fix it!" he said. He pointed at the broken television. "Fix that, too." Then, he walked off.

The Major followed his brother outside into the parking lot; hurried after him as the Colonel headed for his black Cadillac. "Frank," he said, "what are we going to do? Junior already paid the guy."

"The whole twenty-five thousand?"

"He says they insisted," the Major said. "Maybe we can get somebody else?"

"On four hours' notice?"

"What about Clarence Frogletter and his band?" the Major suggested. "They're only two hours away."

The Colonel chuckled. "Last time Frogletter played for us," he said, "Daddy threw peaches at him. Said his banjo playing sounded like a buzz saw, and if he ever came to Buford again, he'd have 'im tarred and feathered."

"I forgot that."

"We're stuck with the comedian," the Colonel said. "Go see 'im. Be nice…but make sure he knows that we don't appreciate the kind of insulting humor he does on the television."

"Okay, I'll do that," the Major said.

"Be nice, now," the Colonel called after his brother.

"Up yours, Frank," the Major muttered to himself.

CHAPTER FOUR

Our adjoining rooms at the Grand Hotel were not "grand," but they were clean. The décor was early 1900s. Each room had a brass bed, a dresser and an armchair. There were no phones or closets.

I started my unpacking, then stopped and strolled into Jackie's room. It was time to address the elephant. His suitcase and wardrobe bag were still on the bed, unopened, and he was slumped down in the armchair in his full dejected mode.

"We've got to back out of this one, Jack," I said. "These people are going to see you up on that stage and get damn angry.

No reaction.

"Are you hearing me?" I said.

"Can you believe that there is no phone in this room?" he said. How are we going to order room service?"

"Jack...."

"Not that you'd want to eat the shit that they probably serve in this piece of shit town," he continued. "Grits...black-eyed peas...horse manure...."

"Listen to me, Jack!" I was ready to grab and throttle him.

"No!" he said. "I'm keepin' the money and doin' the show. That's it!"

We glowered at each other, and then he got up out of the chair. "I'm going to take a shower and a nap," he said.

"Good idea," I said. I retreated to my room and shut the door.

About an hour later, Jackie was in bed, fast asleep, when he became aware of somebody fondling his genitalia.

At first, he thought he was dreaming, but then he abruptly became aware that there was really a hand on his pecker. He sat bolt upright in the bed and saw that that hand belonged to a cute little blonde girl with large breasts, who was in the bed next to him, totally naked.

"Jesus!" Jackie said, jumping out of bed, wearing only a t-shirt and boxer shorts.

The girl seemed surprised and disappointed. "You're not Jake Moss!" she said.

"I know that." Jackie said. "Who the hell are you?"

"This is Jake Moss' room," the girl insisted.

"He couldn't make it," Jackie said, grabbing his pants. "Christ, I knew they started you girls young down here, but… How old are you? Twelve?"

"I'm fourteen."

Jackie fastened his belt. "Are you trying to get me arrested?" he said. "Get the hell out of here!"

The girl suddenly realized that she was fully exposed. "Stop looking at me naked," she demanded. "You're not supposed to see me naked!"

Jackie shrugged; turned his back to her. "Just get out," he said.

The girl grabbed her clothes, jeans and a tank top, and put them back on. "You're just a dirty old man," she said, walking out the door.

"This place just gets better and better," Jackie mumbled.

Downstairs in the lobby, Angie Benedict was behind the check-in desk and Babin was sitting by the window, reading his book, when the Major walked in. Spotting him, Babin closed the book and started to get up, but the Major stopped him with a quick shake of the head that sent the message, "Not now."

"Hello, Bill," Angie Benedict said, looking up from what she was doing. "I bet I know why you're here."

"What's he like?" the Major asked.

"Just like he is on television."

"Shit!" the Major said. "That bad?"

"He's probably a nice person, but today he doesn't appear to be in the best of moods."

"Would you ask him to come down?"

"Sure," she said, starting up the stairs, as the Major wandered over in Babin's direction. She paused on the top step, just out of sight from the lobby.

"So, where are we?" she heard Babin ask, as he pretended to read his book.

"I'm working on it," the Major said.

"Working on it?"

"We'll do it," the Major said, "with or without my brother. I just need some time."

"There is no more time," Babin said. "Tonight."

"Don't worry. You'll have it."

Hearing nothing further, Angie Benedict walked down the hallway toward Jackie's room. She didn't see the cute little blonde girl, now fully, albeit sloppily, dressed, duck into the linen closet in the alcove. "Mr. Moss," she said, tapping on the door of his room, would you come down to the lobby, please? There's somebody who wants to speak to you."

"Sure," Jackie answered, wondering if his visitor was the girl's father with a shotgun.

After Angie Benedict returned to the lobby, the cute little blonde girl emerged from the linen closet and headed for the stairs. She hoped that she could sneak out without anybody seeing her. Moving quickly, she came down the stairs and was halfway across the lobby when she heard her name called. "Billie Jo!"

She turned to see the Major approaching her. "Hi, Uncle Bill," she squeaked.

"What're you doin' here, darlin'?" the Major asked.

"Nuthin'," she said, backing a step toward the front entrance. "Just visitin' a friend."

"A friend?"

"I gotta go, Uncle Bill," she said, hurrying out the door. "Momma's expectin' me."

"What friend?" the Major shouted after her.

After Jackie told me about the underage blonde in his bed, I insisted that I accompany him downstairs to meet whoever had asked to see him. We were in "enemy territory," and somebody had to keep him out of trouble.

"Mr. Moss," Angie Benedict said, "this is Bill Dawson…."

"Major!" Dawson corrected her.

"Sorry," Angie said. "*Major* Dawson. His family's the one that hired you."

"I know you made a mistake," Jackie said, "but I ain't giving back the money."

"Not a problem, Mr. Moss," the Major said, a puzzled expression on his face. He glanced across the lobby at the front entrance. "I'm sure everything will work out for the best."

He and Jackie shook hands, then the Major asked: "You didn't happen to see a little teenage blonde girl upstairs, did you?"

"No, I was asleep in my bed," Jackie said, a little too quickly. "Alone."

The Major studied him for a moment. "Cute child," he said. "Has real big…titties."

"Didn't see no titties."

"That's good," the Major said, "'cause she's my niece."

"Oh!" Jackie chuckled, a bit nervously. "You must be very proud of your niece's…." The Major's cold stare and a slight nudge from me shut him up.

The Major took a deep breath and continued. "I just came by to invite you and…" He looked over at me.

"This is Dave Arthur, my accompanist," Jackie said.

"I just thought that you and Mr. Arthur here might like to join me for a cup of coffee and a piece of pecan pie. Buford is famous for its pecan pie."

"Pecan pie, toilet seats and doo-hickeys," Jackie said. "Wow!"

"'Beg pardon?" the Major said, as I nudged Jackie again.

"Do I call you 'Major'?" Jackie asked, as we headed toward the hotel's front entrance.

"Please do."

"Just don't expect me to salute," Jackie said.

The Major took us to Molly's, a corner restaurant across the street from the hotel. It wasn't quite a coffee shop; more like a small storefront establishment with a counter and a few booths. There were half-dozen customers inside, plus Molly, the fifty-year or so old overweight waitress/owner.

Without asking what we wanted, the Major ordered for all of us: coffee and large wedges of pecan pie. He devoured his piece rather quickly, while both Jackie and I gave up on our insipid servings after a single bite.

"We want you to do your regular act, Mr. Moss," the Major said, savoring the final morsel of his pie. "We just don't want you to insult people."

"That *is* my act," Jackie said. "Insulting people."

"You're a comedian," the Major said. "Don't you tell jokes?"

"No, I insult people," Jackie said. "I have insulted presidents, kings, movie stars, sports figures…. People like it when I insult them. They consider it an honor."

They don't get mad?" the Major asked. "They don't punch you out?"

"Of course not," Jackie said. "Well, Sinatra did once, but Frank has a hot temper."

"Well," the Major said, "we in Buford have hot tempers, too, Mr. Moss. I'd be careful if I were you." He slid out of the booth. "Enjoy your pie." Calling to Molly, he headed for the door. "Put that on my tab," he said.

"Sure thing," she said.

I looked at Jackie. "That was a threat."

"I know."

"Jack, let's give back the money and leave."

"No. I got a show to do tonight."

Molly waddled over to our booth, a broad smile on her face. "So, how did you like my pecan pie?" she asked.

"Incredible," Jackie said. "Absolutely incredible."

CHAPTER FIVE

The General lived in a white, mid-sized Colonial-style mansion that could have used a new paint job.

The General himself was a Colonel Saunders look-a-like; white beard and mustache, dressed in his full Confederate uniform. Wheelchair bound, Alfred, his oversized black male nurse constantly at his side, the frail ninety-year-old gentleman was on oxygen and only slightly aware of the activity going on around him. He sat on the back porch, a glass of bourbon in his hand, grunting at the guests who approached him to pay homage.

Virtually the entire town was in attendance at the General's birthday party. Everybody was dressed in their Sunday best, though the fashion styles were a few years out-of-date.

Ham, yams, fried chicken, grits, pecan pie and other Southern dishes sat on the lush green lawn atop a linen-covered buffet table that ran the length of the porch, and was attended by a half dozen or so black servers in white jackets. Circular tables with chairs were set up in front of the buffet, so that the guests could eat and enjoy the show, which, apparently, was to be presented on the back porch, since that's where they'd set the upright piano.

Of course, the entire Dawson clan was there: the Colonel with his wife, Arlene, an attractive, well-endowed redhead in her late thirties and their daughter, Billie Jo; the Major, with his near fifty-year-old wife, Violet, a bleached blonde, also with oversized breasts, who was once the town's beauty queen, but now wore far too much make-up and was never without a drink in her hand. People at the party pretty much ignored her, as they did with the Corporal, the Major's son, who, by now, everybody knew was responsible for the Jackie/Jake mix-up.

"He's *really* on television?" Billie Jo asked her cousin.

"Movies, too," the Corporal said. "He don't sing. He just tells jokes."

"He *is* kinda funny-lookin'," the girl said, "and so old."

The Corporal just shook his head and took another sip of his beer. "Jake, Jackie, Jakie," he said. "How do you tell the difference?"

Browsing the buffet table was Charlie Buford, the hefty, balding local sheriff and the last surviving member of the town's founding family. He was chatting with wiry, white-haired Abner Whitcomb, the town's only attorney, who made his living by drawing up wills, simple contracts, handling probates and also serving as justice of the peace. Both men were in their sixties.

Paul Babin was also there, but he pretty much kept to himself.

"What's with you and Babin?" the Colonel asked his brother after he noticed the visitor from Prague.

"Nothing," the Major said. "He's a potential buyer. I invited him to the party."

"You've set him straight on that matter?"

"Yeah," the Major muttered. "Sure."

"Good," the Colonel said, "'cause I hate end runs."

"Not a problem," the Major said, turning away from his brother and catching his sister-in-law's eye.

Arlene Dawson winked at him.

While this gathering was in progress behind the mansion, Edward chauffeured tuxedo-clad Jackie and me up to the front of the house. I really didn't want to be there.

"Think we should leave the motor running?" Jackie quipped, as we stepped out of the Cadillac.

"Just behave," I said.

"Yes, Daddy." Jackie said.

"This way, gentlemen," Edward said, leading us through the front door of the mansion.

The house had one of those circular staircases, like they had in *Gone With The Wind*, and Jackie couldn't resist the temptation. "Frankly, my dear," he mimicked in his best Clark Gable voice, "I don't give a damn."

"That's very good, Mr. Moss," Edward chuckled.

"Yeah?" Jackie said. "You should hear my Vivien Leigh."

Edward chuckled again. "Oh, Mr. Moss," he said, shaking his head and starting up the stairs.

"Fiddle dee dee! Fiddle dee dee!" Angie Benedict said with a mock Georgia accent, as she stood inside the French doors that led to the back porch. She was dressed in a smart bare shoulder black cocktail dress that was bound to turn heads, particularly in Buford.

Jackie looked at her and beamed. "Why, Miss Scarlett," he said. "You do a better Vivien Leigh than I do."

"Well, thank you, sir," she said with a slight curtsy. "I just wanted to wish you a good show, Mr. Moss. What is it they say? 'Break a leg'?"

"Thank you, Miss....? Angie, isn't it?"

"That's right," she said. "I saw you perform in New York once."

"Really?" Jackie said, moving closer to her. "I thought you were born, bred and firmly planted in Buford."

"No," she replied. "I've seen the outside world. I moved back here after my folks died. Took over the family business."

"That's quite an outfit you're wearing," Jackie said, surveying her dress. "Maybe we could have a drink after...?"

"Who knows?" Angie Benedict said with a wink. She headed across the large tiled entry hall toward what was, apparently, a guest bathroom.

"Who knows?" Jackie said to himself, watching her sashay away.

Edward interrupted the moment. "They're goin' to serve your supper in one of the upstairs bed-sitting rooms," he said. "You'll be comfortable there 'til it's time for the show."

"Fine," Jackie said.

Edward led us upstairs to a large bedroom, complete with four-poster bed and chaise lounge. A small table in the center of the room was set with our meal; fried chicken, mashed potatoes and greens.

Edward pointed to a bell cord by the bed. "You gentlemen just ring if you need anything more," he said.

"Thank you, Edward," I said.

Edward had no sooner shut the door behind him than Jackie looked at the food and scowled. "Wouldn't you know it?" he said. "Fried chicken."

"So?"

"Great for the cholesterol."

"Suffer," I said.

We doffed our tuxedo jackets, sat down and started to eat. Actually, the chicken was pretty good. I could tell that Jackie liked it, but he wasn't about to admit it. After he'd finished devouring a second chicken breast, he started discussing the act. "So," he said, "you play a little 'Dixie,' a little 'Battle Hymn of the Republic'..."

"You really think that's a good idea?" I said.

"Yes, I think it's a good idea," he snapped, and then he softened his tone. "Dave, when we were kids and Butch Franklin and his gang of bullies beat up on me....What would I do?"

"You'd bleed."

"That, too," he said, "but I'd also insult Butch....Funny."

"And, he'd hit you again."

"Yeah, but then I'd insult him again...funny...and his gang would start laughing...*at him*. And, then he'd have to

laugh, because if he didn't, he'd really look like a *schmuck*....
Don't you remember? Butch and I became buddies."

"Jack," I said, "those people downstairs are not going to
become your buddies."

"Dave," he said, "play the piano. I'll do the jokes."

I decided to shut up.

"I need a beer or something to get rid of the taste of this
crap," he said, standing and heading for the door. "You want
one?"

"Sure."

"I'll call Edward."

I pointed to the bell cord. "You can ring the bell for him,"
I said.

"Who am I? Quasimodo?" he said. "I'll give him a
shout."

Jackie opened the door and stepped out into the hallway.
"Edwa..." he started to call, and then he stopped.

Leaning against a doorway on the opposite wall was the
Major and an attractive redhead that, at the moment, Jackie
didn't know was Arlene Dawson, the Major's sister-in-law. Her
skirt was hiked-up; the Major's pants were at half-mast. The
couple was "doing it."

They paused and looked at Jackie, and for once in his life,
he was at a loss for words. He smiled, gave the Major a quick
salute, did an about face and retreated back into our makeshift
dressing room.

"Did you find Edward?" I asked, as he shut the door.

"No," Jackie said. "The Major."

"The Major?"

"Yeah," Jackie said. "He was standing at attention."

Jack had barely finished telling me about his encounter
when the door opened and the Major, pants up and buckled,
walked into the room. "Mr. Moss," he said, apparently trying
to keep calm.

"Not to worry about it, Major," Jackie interrupted with a wink. "What happens in Buford stays in Buford."

I didn't like the look in the Major's eye. "What does that mean?" he said.

"It means," Jackie said, "I didn't see a fucking thing."

"See that you didn't."

The Major scowled at Jackie, then departed, slamming the door behind him.

"Was that a threat?" Jackie asked.

"Just let it go," I said.

"I don't like threats," Jackie said, and I knew we were in for trouble.

CHAPTER SIX

The show was destined to be a disaster. Any idiot could tell that from the start.

The party guests were seated at their tables. As the Major mounted the porch to introduce Jackie, I slipped out through the French doors and seated myself at the upright piano. "Folks," the Major said to the group, "we got some entertainment here for you tonight…. It's not what you expected…."

There were a couple of audible groans from the audience. The Major ignored them. "But," he continued, "we've all seen this Jackie Moss on television, and he's a funny man."

I caught Jackie out of the corner of my eye, standing just inside the French doors. He did not look happy about an introduction that sounded more like an apology.

"So," the Major finished, "let's all welcome Jackie Moss."

There was mild applause, as I started playing Jackie's introduction music. The people in the front part of the audience were not smiling. Indeed, many of them had their arms folded and, as Jackie would remark later, it looked as if we were at an undertaker's convention.

Yet, beaming his stock entrance smile, Jackie bounded onto the stage and began singing his opening number, "Let Me Entertain You" with his own inimitable lyrics.

Over at the side of the porch where he was sitting, the general turned to Alfred, his male nurse, and in a loud voice, demanded, "Who the hell is that?"

Jackie was annoyed. He tried to ignore the General. He continued to sing.

"That's not Jake Moss!" the General said, even louder than before.

Jackie turned to the General and quipped, "He's entertaining at a bris in Brooklyn." He returned to his singing.

That didn't stop the Colonel Saunders look-alike. He pointed at Jackie and shouted, "What's *he* doing up there?"

"I'M SINGING A SONG," Jackie crooned, turning to the General and improvising a lyric that matched the tune I was playing.

"Well, I don't like it," the General said.

Jackie stopped singing. I stopped playing and held my breath.

"Well," Jackie said, "I don't like your 'original recipe,' Colonel. My bubbe makes better chicken than you."

"It's General!" the old man said.

"Oh?" Jackie said, moving over to the General's table. "I heard you got busted!"

The audience had grown quiet; a few murmurings and whisperings. They knew something was coming.

The General's face had turned crimson. "I'll bust you, you…" he said, then he bopped Jackie on the forehead with his cane. It wasn't a hard strike, but it caused Jackie to stagger a step backwards.

There were gasps of shock from the crowd. The only thought that came to my mind was, "Oh, shit!"

Jackie felt his head. The General had not drawn blood. He stared at the General for several seconds. Then he said, "Sorry, old timer. Sinatra hits harder."

That broke the tension. There was a wave of nervous laughter from the audience, except from Angie Benedict. She was laughing so hard that people turned and looked at her.

The General wasn't laughing. He raised his cane to throw at Jackie, but Alfred moved in and took it away from him. "You just take it easy, General, sir," he said. "You don't want to soil yourself again."

That seemed to calm the old man, but he continued to glower at Jackie.

I looked at Jackie. He was angry, and when Jackie was angry, he threw caution to the wind. "Everybody enjoy the dinner?" he asked the audience.

Most everybody nodded.

"Actually," he continued, "the chozzerai they fed us upstairs wasn't bad. The dog ate it...before he died."

There were mild groans from the audience.

"Look folks," Jackie continued, "I'm sorry I'm not the putz with the Stetson and the guitar you were hoping for, but the schmuck that booked me made the mistake, not me."

For a moment, it seemed that everybody in the crowd turned and scowled at the Corporal.

"So," Jackie said, "I'm here. Let's make the best of it."

There were a few disgruntled nods and murmurings from the audience.

"If you like," Jackie persisted, "I can sing 'Dixie'... 'Marching Through Georgia'...."

"No, that's the wrong one, isn't it?" he said to me.

He turned back to the audience: "Actually, I love the South. It's a beautiful place....I love the movies about the South...*The Birth of a Nation*...*Gone With the Wind*...*To Kill a Mockingbird*... *Deliverance*...."

There were a couple of groans and even a "Boo" from the audience.

"And, Buford," Jackie went on. "The population may be small, and you may be stuck up here in the mountains, but it's towns like yours that make the South great....You are a pillar of American industry....You make toilet seats....What could be more basic to the American way of life?...And, you make doo-hickeys for the Navy...What a combination!...What

American wouldn't want to sit on his toilet seat and fiddle with his doo-hickey?"

There were a few mild chuckles from the from the audience and some groans, but Angie Benedict, once again, laughed out loud before she stopped herself.

And, the Colonel's jailbait daughter, Billie Jo, also seemed to be enjoying Jackie's performance; a big grin on her face. The Colonel and the Major, on the other hand, did not appear to be happy campers.

"Talk about toilets," Jackie whispered to me out of the side of his mouth before he went on.

And, that's the way it went for the next forty-five minutes. A few chuckles, several groans, no guffaws, except from Angie Benedict and, occasionally, Billie Jo.

Jackie finished his closing number. There was some polite applause, then while I played his exit music, he walked back through the French doors where Edward was waiting for him. "I enjoyed your show, Mr. Moss," our driver said.

"You're the only one," Jackie grumbled.

"I guess I'd better take you back to the hotel."

"Just long enough to get our stuff," Jackie said, seeing me walk in from the porch. "Then take us to the airport."

"It's too dangerous to drive the mountain at night," Edward said. "That'll have to wait 'til morning."

"Mr. Moss...," the Colonel's voice boomed, as he and the Major entered the room.

"Yes?" Jackie muttered.

"I'm Frank Dawson...."

"Dawson?"

"You can call me 'Colonel'."

I knew Jackie was tempted to make a quip, but I nudged him and he shut up. "And, what can I do for you…Colonel?" he asked.

"We'd like you to come back out and take a picture with the family."

"Oh, that's extra," Jackie said before I could nudge him again.

"I beg your pardon?" the Colonel said.

Jackie exhaled loudly. "Okay, why not?" he said. "Just don't have me stand next to the old guy with the cane."

"I'm very sorry about that," the Colonel said, as we walked back onto the porch. "But, my daddy, the General…He's not always himself these days."

"So, who is he? Buford Pusser?" Jackie quipped, referring to the bat wielding Tennessee sheriff immortalized by the movie, *Walking Tall*.

The Colonel's response was deadpan. "That's very funny, Mr. Moss."

"Very funny," the Major agreed, also pokerfaced.

The family was gathered on the porch, seated or standing around the General, who still had Alfred at his side. A photographer was positioning them for the picture.

"He's still here…?" the General growled when he saw Jackie.

"It's okay, General, sir," Alfred assured his charge.

The General was undeterred. "If I was younger," he shouted at Jackie, "I'd take you out into the woods and give you a good whippin'."

"Glad you liked the show," Jackie said.

"And then, maybe I'd hang you from the nearest tree."

"Daddy, behave yourself," the Colonel said, then to Jackie, "I apologize, sir."

"Okay," Jackie said, "let's just take the picture, and…"

The Colonel started on the left to introduce the family: "This is my sister-in-law, Violet, my nephew, Billy, Junior…."

"Hi, ya all," Jackie said, feigning interest.

"My wife, Arlene…" the Colonel continued.

"*Your* wife…" Jackie said, doing a slight double-take.

The redhead smiled at him, like ice.

Jackie glanced at the Major.

He was smiling with daggers.

"Nice to meet you, Mrs. Dawson," Jackie said with a broad smile on his face.

"And, this is my daughter, Billie Jo," the Colonel went on.

Jackie saw the cute little blonde girl with large breasts and blanched. "Right…," he stammered.

Billie Jo grabbed his hand and held it. "I just think you were so funny, Mr. Moss," she said. "I had no idea who you were."

Jackie withdrew his had from the young siren's grasp. "Can we take the picture, now?" he said to the Colonel.

"Yes," the Colonel said with a scowl. "I think we'd better."

They took the picture without further delay, and then Edward drove us back to the hotel. He said he would pick us up at eight the next morning and drive us to the Little Rock airport.

Jackie was still wide-awake and wanted to play some Gin Rummy, but I was tired and wanted to go to bed. Besides, I'd had enough of his grouchiness on this trip and I knew if we played cards, I'd get a lot more of it because I could always beat him.

I don't know how long I'd been asleep. I do know that I was dreaming that I was Randolph Scott and I was in the desert, about to face down Lee Marvin in a gunfight.

The "shot" I fired that brought Marvin down half woke me up. It sounded and felt so real, but then I dozed off again.

The next thing that I remember is that there was a loud pounding on my hotel room door. I opened my eyes and saw several citizens of Buford standing around my bed, looking down at me.

They were not smiling.

CHAPTER SEVEN

"Better get your clothes on, son," Sheriff Buford said, pushing his way through the group of disgruntled townsfolk who were surrounding my bed.

I looked at my watch. It read 2:15. "What's going on?" I asked, still half asleep.

"We'll talk about that down at my office. Now, put on your pants."

"Why don't we just take 'im out to the old oak tree and be done with it?" some skinny guy in a plaid shirt, dirty jeans and a three-day growth on his face piped up.

"Archie, you stop that kind of talk," the sheriff said. "We ain't lynched nobody in Buford for near twenty years."

"Lynched?" I stammered, quickly pulling on my pants.

"Don't worry, son," the sheriff said. "You'll get a fair trial. You just come with me."

"What 'trial'?" I said, as he took me by the arm and led me, shoes in my hand, through the small mob and out into the hallway.

There was what looked like streaks of fresh blood on the burgundy wallpaper, and the door to Jackie's room was open, but he wasn't inside.

"Where's Jackie?" I asked the sheriff.

"I got 'im down at the jail," he said. "It's for his own safety 'til the trial."

"You keep talking about a trial," I said, as we descended the stairs. "What trial?"

The lobby was filled with even more townsfolk. I didn't like the way they were looking at me.

"You just keep movin', son," the sheriff said, as we pushed our way through the crowd.

"You'll pay for this!" somebody shouted.

"Damn right!" bellowed somebody else.

I caught a glimpse of Angie Benedict behind the check-in desk. She was talking on the phone, a troubled look on her face.

It seemed like the rest of Buford's entire population was gathered on the street outside the hotel. They all looked angry, too. I thought I saw somebody in the crowd waving a rope.

"Just keep movin', son," the sheriff said.

As he put me into the back seat of this mid-1960s Ford police car, I noticed Paul Babin standing by the hotel entrance. He appeared to be amused by my plight.

The sheriff got behind the wheel; made a U-turn. The crowd…or mob…continued to glower at us, as we headed down the hill.

"Would you please tell me what's going on?" I said, finally putting on my shoes.

"Well," the sheriff said, "it looks like your friend, Jackie Moss, shot Colonel Dawson."

"What!?!"

"Colonel's at the clinic right now. He's unconscious. Don't know if he's gonna pull through or not."

"Are you crazy?" I said. "Why would Jackie shoot the Colonel?"

"Dunno."

"He doesn't even have a gun."

"The gun was in his hand. And, we got witnesses."

"Witnesses?"

"The Major saw it. Also, that Babin fella from Europe."

I couldn't believe what I was hearing. "What…what did Jackie say?"

"Didn't say much of anything," the sheriff said. "He was unconscious, too. Said somebody hit him."

The jailhouse was like something out of an old television Western, like *Gunsmoke*.

The pair of prisoner cells, with iron bars from floor to ceiling, were against the right wall of the large single room, while the sheriff's wooden desk, a gun rack filled with rifles and shotguns, a corkboard of "Wanted" posters, and all the other paraphernalia one would expect to find in such a setting, were against the other.

With its wood paneling and floor, it was actually a rather warm room, but Jackie didn't think so. When I was brought in, he was sitting in one of the cells, shivering in his t-shirt and boxer shorts. "Dave!" he shouted, hurrying over to the bars.

"Jackie," I said, "are you okay?"

"I'm standing here, half naked, freezing my tuchis off in a jail cell, and you're asking me if I'm okay?"

"Where's his clothes?" I said to the sheriff.

"We didn't have time to get 'im dressed," Buford said. "The boys were gettin' pretty ugly, and we had to get 'im out of the hotel fast."

"Get him his clothes," I demanded, figuring that showing some authority couldn't put me in any worse of a position than I was in already. After all, they could only lynch me once.

What was I thinking?

Buford turned to his deputy, a stubby fellow with a three-day beard and swollen nose. "Wilbur," he said, "get Mr. Moss here a blanket, then go over to the hotel and get him some clothes."

"Sure thing, sheriff," Wilbur said, heading for a closet toward the back part of the jailhouse.

"We'll get 'im fixed up right away," Buford said.

"That's fine," I said. "Now, I want to call our attorney."

"Yeah!" Jackie said. "Call Ray. He'll know what to do."

"Look, son," Buford said, "we don't need no big city attorneys comin' in here and confusin' things. Abner Whitcomb is a fine lawyer, our justice o' the peace, and he can handle this just fine."

"We want our own representation," I insisted.

"Yeah," Jackie agreed. "I don't want no hick lawyer."

Wilbur, by this time, had retrieved a dark gray blanket from the closet and handed it to Jackie through the bars. "You sure this don't have fleas?" Jackie said.

"My dog, Rufus, don't have no fleas," Wilbur said with a snarl.

"I'm happy to know that," Jackie said.

"Wilbur," Buford said, "get over to the hotel and get him his clothes."

"Okay, sheriff." Wilbur headed toward the front door, but then turned back to Jackie.

"I saw you on the TV," he said with a big almost empty-mouthed grin. "You were kinda funny."

"Thank you," Jackie scowled. He pointed to the deputy's maw. "Nice tooth."

Wilbur nodded, not quite sure how to take Jackie's quip, then went out through the front door.

Outside, I could hear the angry voices of the growing mob.

"Sheriff," I said, "do you mind if I talk to my friend?"

"Just don't try nuthin' funny."

"Don't worry," Jackie said. "I do the jokes, not him."

The sheriff sat behind his desk, and I moved up next to Jackie's cell. "What happened?" I whispered to him.

"I don't know," he said, gingerly wrapping the blanket around him. "I was in bed. I heard some shouting outside my door. I went to tell them to shut the fuck up and somebody slugged me."

"You didn't see who did it?

"No," he said. "The next thing I knew, I was lying in this cell in my underwear, and they're sayin' that I shot somebody."

"The Colonel?"

"Yeah, him."

"This has got to be a frame," I said.

"You're telling me?"

The door opened, and I could hear the crowd outside getting louder. The Major and Abner Whitcomb entered. Both had changed from their party attire and were dressed more casually. I didn't like the grim expressions on their faces.

"How's the Colonel?" Buford asked.

"Still unconscious," the Major said. "Nurse is still workin' on him. A helicopter's gonna come; fly 'im into a Little Rock hospital in the morning."

Whitcomb saw me standing outside of Jackie's cell. "Shouldn't he be locked up?" he said.

"I wasn't sure what to do with him," Buford said.

"He could be an accomplice," the Major said.

"Accomplice to what?" I said, moving over toward them.

"Just watch it, son," Buford said, resting his hand on his sidearm. "You don't want to make it worse for yourself."

"We want an attorney," I demanded.

"That's why Abner's here," Buford said. "I told you he's a fine lawyer."

"You'll get everything that's comin' to you," Whitcomb said.

"That's what worries me," I said. "The law says I'm entitled to a phone call."

"What law is that?" Whitcomb said.

I couldn't believe what I'd just heard.

"Don't you guys watch television?" Jackie said.

"Son," the sheriff said, "up here in Buford, we kinda do stuff our own way."

"Oy!" Jackie said.

"Tell me something," I said. "Why would Jackie shoot The Colonel? He just met the man last night."

"Maybe my brother found out about him and Billie Jo," said The Major.

"Billie Jo?"

"The Colonel's daughter. My niece. She's under age."

"I never touched that girl," Jackie shouted. "She snuck into my room when I was asleep."

"Shut up, Jackie," I said.

"I figure that my brother came over to confront Mr. Moss, and…."

"Jackie doesn't even have a gun," I said.

"I don't know," The Major said with a shrug. "Maybe he grabbed my brother's."

"Even if he did," I said, "that would be self-defense."

"That's for a jury to determine, son," Whitcomb said. He gestured to Buford, "Sheriff."

Buford grabbed the ring of cell keys off his desk. "Now," he said to me, "why don't you just step into the cell next to your friend there while we figure out what we're goin' to do next?" He rested his hand on his sidearm again.

"You know," I said, walking toward the empty cell, "Jackie Moss is a very famous man…."

"I even performed at The White House for the President," Jackie added.

"If something happens to him…"

"Don't give them any ideas," Jackie said.

"Nuthin's gonna happen to him that ain't within the law," Whitcomb said. "Right now, the charge is 'attempted murder'…and 'statuary rape'."

"It's 'statutory'," Jackie said. "This guy's a regular Clarence Darrow."

"Let's just hope that it don't get any worse," the sheriff said. He locked me inside the cell, then walked over to confer with Whitcomb and The Major.

"We gotta get out of here," Jackie whispered. "We gotta get a hold of Ray."

I motioned for him to keep quiet, so that I could hear what Buford and the others were saying.

"The piano player's right, you know," The Major said. "This Moss fella is pretty famous. We gotta be careful how we handle this."

"He'll get a fair trial," Whitcomb said.

"And then what?" The Major said. "We gonna string him up?"

"Once again, that's for the jury to decide," Whitcomb said. "Whatever we do, it'll be legal."

"Yeah," Buford said, "we don't need no tree. We can build a gallows, nice and legal."

Jackie looked at me, aghast. "The Colonel's not even dead," he said, "and they're already building the gallows?"

"You're missing the point," The Major said to Buford and Whitcomb. "As much as I'd like to, we can't try him here."

"Why not?" Buford said.

"If he doesn't show up tomorrow or the next day, Moss' people are gonna start lookin' for him, and when they find out what's happened, our town is gonna 'explode'. We're gonna be invaded by newspapers...the Feds...."

"Could be good for business," Whitcomb said.

"It won't be good for business," The Major snapped. "We don't need that kind of publicity...And, I don't want the F.B.I. snoopin' around The Factory."

"What are you suggesting?" Whitcomb asked.

"We gotta take these two into Little Rock," The Major said. "Let the state attorney try the case."

"Damn it, Bill," Whitcomb said to The Major, "I was looking forward to tryin' this case."

"I'm sorry Abner, but..."

"I haven't had a good case to try since Tad Chandler's mule kicked Amos Griffin in the balls."

"What did you do to the mule," Jackie called out. "Hang 'im?"

"Jackie, shut up," I whispered.

"No," Whitcomb said. "We castrated 'im."

Jackie grimaced.

"He was a good mule," Whitcomb said.

"Just be quiet," I said to Jackie. "Let me handle it."

"Then, handle it."

"Gentlemen," I said, "The Major's right. If you don't conduct this the right way, this town could wind up under martial law."

"We don't want no martial law," Buford said. "Remember what happened in Mississippi?"

"Don't worry about it, Mr. Arthur," The Major said. "We're gonna take you into Little Rock."

Jackie and I both breathed a sigh of relief.

"But with that crowd out there, we just gotta figure out a safe way to do it."

CHAPTER EIGHT

"I'm wondering," Jackie said.

He was wearing his tux jacket and pants, the only clothing that Wilbur, the deputy, had retrieved from the hotel.

"Wondering what?" I said.

It was morning. We'd been sitting in our adjoining cells for over four hours, waiting for The Major, Abner Whitcomb and Sheriff Buford to figure out a way to get us to Little Rock without causing the townsfolk to riot. They'd left about four-thirty to make arrangements, and from the sounds outside, it seemed like the mob had pretty much dissipated.

At least, I hoped so.

The only other person in the jailhouse was Wilbur, and he was sitting behind the desk, snoring away.

"I was wondering," Jackie continued, "if The Major had anything to do with The Colonel getting shot."

"Cain and Abel?"

"Something like that," Jackie said.

"Why would he shoot his own brother?"

"Maybe The Colonel found out The Major was shtuping his wife."

"Could be," I pondered. "But, if that's the reason, why would he come down to the hotel to confront his brother? Why not the office? His home? Someplace else?"

"You expect me to have all the answers?" Jackie said.

"The story about you and his daughter makes more sense, but…."

"You know what happened there," Jackie said. "Whose side are you on?"

"Isn't it interesting," I said, "that The Major was the one pushing for us to be taken to Little Rock?"

"Why is that interesting?"

"It's like he wants the whole thing to go away."

"Away where?" Jackie said.

"You're a famous person," I said, thinking aloud. "If you get tried in Little Rock, that's where the focus of the case shifts. That's where the press will be."

"That's what the Major was talking about," Jackie said. "They don't want the press…or the F.B.I.…."

"Exactly," I said. "They don't want the F.B.I. snooping around The Factory."

"It must have something to do with the 'doo-hickey'," Jackie said.

"I'm thinking that, for whatever reason The Colonel was at the hotel last night, it had nothing to do with his daughter or his wife."

"Maybe somebody was trying to steal his doo-hickey?"

"Maybe," I said, "but we've got to come up with a better term than that."

"What's wrong with 'doo-hickey'?" Jackie said with a smile.

It was the first time he'd smiled, since this mess had started. I joined him.

Our moment was interrupted by a knock on the jailhouse's front door.

Wilbur, somewhat startled, came awake. "What?" he said.

Another knock, this one louder.

"Okay, I'm comin'," Wilbur said, getting up from the desk and heading for the door. "Who is it?"

"Angie Benedict."

Wilbur fumbled with the keys. "Sheriff's not here, Miss Benedict," he said, opening the door slightly.

Angie was dressed in gray slacks and a plaid shirt. She was carrying a large brown shopping bag. "I brought you and your prisoners some breakfast."

"That sure is nice of you, Miss Benedict," Wilbur said, letting her inside, and then locking the door behind her. "I am pretty hungry."

"So are we," Jackie said.

"She winked at Jackie, then pulled a sandwich wrapped in aluminum foil out of the bag and handed it to Wilbur. "I hope you like fried egg sandwiches," she said.

"Sure do," the deputy replied. "I'll make some coffee." He headed over toward a hot plate and coffee pot in the corner of the room.

"Okay if I feed your prisoners?" she asked.

"Just so you don't slip 'em any guns or files," he said with a guffaw. He started to prepare the coffee pot.

Angie Benedict chuckled. "Oh, I wouldn't do that," she said. She moved over to our cells. "How are you?" she asked Jackie.

"How do you think I am?" Then, he whispered: "You don't have a gun or a file, do you?"

"No," she said, handing us our sandwiches through the bars.

"I didn't shoot The Colonel," Jackie said. "I didn't shoot anybody."

"I know," Angie Benedict said. "But, this is Buford."

"No, it's not," Jackie said. "It's *The Twilight Zone*."

"Is the mob still out there?" I asked.

"They're gone," Angie Benedict said. "Just a couple of guys hanging around."

"Would you call my manager, Ray Crystal?" Jackie whispered. He's in Los Angeles."

"I will when the outside phone lines are back up."

"The phone lines are down?" I said.

"When you live in the mountains," Angie said, "that happens every now and then."

"That's pretty convenient," Jackie said. "So, nobody outside of this place knows what's happening?"

"I don't think so," Angie Benedict said.

"That's not good," I said. "We were hoping that Ray Crystal could have legal representation meet us when we got to Little Rock."

"They're transferring you to Little Rock?" Angie Benedict said.

"Yeah," Jackie said. "The Major's arranging it."

She glanced back at Wilbur, who was still engaged in making the coffee. "I don't think that's a good idea," she whispered to us.

"Why isn't that a good idea?" Jackie said.

"I don't think it's safe," she said, just as the front door of the jail opened and The Major and Sheriff Buford walked in.

"Hello, Angie," The Major said. "What are you doing here?"

"I brought breakfast," she said, moving away from the cells.

"That's very thoughtful of you," The Major said, a questioning expression on his face.

"Fried egg sandwiches," Wilbur said.

"They can eat theirs on the road," the sheriff said. "We're transferring 'em to Little Rock."

"Little Rock?" Angie Benedict said.

""Yeah," The Major said, "if that mob forms again, we might not be able to handle them."

"You're going to drive them?"

"How else would we get them there?"

"Aren't you flying your brother out in a helicopter?" Angie Benedict said. "Why can't they go with him?"

"First, there's not enough room in the chopper," The Major said, "and, under the circumstances, do you really think that would be appropriate?"

"Probably not."

"Why would you even care?"

"They shot The Colonel," Buford said. "They raped his daughter."

"I did not!" Jackie shouted. "You keep making this stuff up! Next, you're gonna say that I shot President Kennedy."

"We can look into that, too," the sheriff said.

Jackie and I exchanged a glance. We were both speechless.

"They said they didn't do it," Angie Benedict said.

"Well, that's what trials are for." The Major said. "Again, why would you even care?"

"Because I don't think they're guilty."

"Whatever," The Major said. He gestured to Buford.

"Miss Benedict," the sheriff said, opening the jailhouse door, "you'd better go."

"Why can't she stay?" Jackie said.

The sheriff pointed to the door. "We gotta get these fellas out of here before the mob forms again," he said.

Angie Benedict started to object, but then, I guess, thought better of it. She walked out of the jailhouse without saying another word.

"Make that phone call!" Jackie shouted after her.

The sheriff locked the door behind her.

"What phone call is that?" The Major asked.

"I told her to call my bookie," Jack said. "I want to bet a hundred on Rocket Boy in the third."

"You're a very funny man, Mr. Moss," The Major said with a dour face.

"So, what's going on here?" I asked.

"We've made arrangements to get you out of town and down to Little Rock," The Major said.

"What arrangements?" I asked.

"A business associate is going to drive you," The Major said. "He was planning to leave town this morning anyway, so nobody will be the wiser."

"Then what?"

"We spoke to the state police. They'll meet you just outside of Little Rock and take it from there."

"The Arkansas State Police?" I said.

"I spoke to them personally just before I came here," The Major said.

"But, I thought…," Jackie started to say, then realized that he'd better keep quiet.

"Thought what?" The Major said.

"I don't know," Jackie said. "Maybe it would be safer if we stayed here and let the state police come to us. What do you think?"

"Yes," I said. "That might be safer."

"That's not an option," The Major said, looking at the sheriff.

Buford stepped forward with the cell keys. "Okay, gents," he said, "we can do this the hard way or the easy way."

"There's a difference?" Jackie said.

"I'm talkin' with or without hand and leg irons."

"I'd prefer without," Jackie said.

This didn't sound quite kosher to me. "You're telling us," I said, "that you're willing to transport us without any restraints?"

"Where you gonna run?" the sheriff said. "You're in the Ozark Mountains. It's filled with bears, wolves and moon shiners. You city boys wouldn't stand a chance."

"Actually," Jackie said, "I could use a little moonshine right now."

"Save us the cost of a hangin'," the sheriff said with a chuckle.

"That bad, huh?" Jackie said.

"You wouldn't believe," the sheriff said. He unlocked my cell door and motioned me to step out. "Don't forget your sandwiches."

I didn't like this. Considering Angie Benedict's warning and the fact that I'd seen so many Western movies, I was fully expecting that somebody was about to yell "Jail Break," then shoot us in the back.

On the other hand, with Jackie's celebrity, such as it was, an incident like that would certainly raise a lot of questions and shine an unwanted spotlight on the town of Buford and its factory.

Still, I didn't like it.

"Car's waitin' out back," the sheriff said, leading us to the barred rear door of the jailhouse.

"You boys'll get a fair trial in Little Rock," The Major said, as the door was unlocked.

Outside in the alley behind the jail was a two-door gray BMW, and leaning against it, dressed in his dark fashionable suit, was Paul Babin. Otherwise, the alley was empty.

Babin smiled when he saw us.

"What the hell!" Jackie said. "What are you doing here?"

"He's driving you to Little Rock," The Major said.

Jackie and I exchanged a glance. Again, we were speechless.

"Do not worry," Babin said. "I am a very good driver."

"We packed up your luggage," The Major said. "It's in the trunk."

Babin opened the door on the passenger side of car. "Please get in the rear seat and keep low," he said. "When we are out of town, you can sit up and be comfortable."

Jackie and I hesitated.

"Do what the man says," the sheriff said.

"Please," Babin said with a smile.

There was something about that smile that made me nervous.

Nevertheless, with the sheriff's hand resting on his side-arm, Jackie and I climbed into the back seat of the BMW and crouched down on the floor. It was definitely not very comfortable.

Babin closed the door behind us, and then walked around the car and slid behind the wheel. He started the engine.

"Don't you give this man no trouble," the sheriff said.

"They won't," The Major said. "They know what's good for them."

The BMW moved forward out of the alley and onto the street.

On the floor, Jackie and I couldn't see anything or anybody through the windows. With one hand holding the rear seat and the other grasping the back of the front, we crouched on our knees, our faces less than a foot apart, staring at each other.

"Isn't this romantic?" Jackie sang.

I forced a smile, but my mind was racing. I wondered where Babin was *really* taking us.

"You can sit up, now," Babin said after we'd been driving for about ten minutes.

We clambered up onto the rear seat and saw that we had left the town of Buford. We were driving on a dirt road through a wooded area.

"This isn't the way we came into town." I said.

"No, it isn't." Jackie agreed.

"You gentlemen are very observant," Babin said, looking at us through the rearview mirror. "We are going by a different route."

"To Little Rock?" I said.

"All roads lead to Little Rock," Babin replied, flashing his disturbing smile. "This one is less traveled. We don't want the people from Buford spotting us, do we?"

I looked at Jackie.

He looked at me.

We read each other's mind.

We both knew were in *deep shit*.

"Where, exactly, are we meeting the Arkansas State Police?" I asked.

"We're not," Babin said.

"*We're not!?!*" Jackie said.

Babin chuckled. "Do not worry, my friends," he said. "All has been arranged."

"What's been arranged?" Jackie said.

"About a half mile down this road is a car," Babin said. "I believe it is a Chevrolet. The keys are inside, and you will drive this Chevrolet down this dirt road until you reach the main road down the mountain."

"I don't understand," Jackie said.

"You will drive to the Little Rock Airport and fly back to Los Angeles."

"So, you're letting us go?" I said.

"I still don't understand," Jackie said.

"Unfortunately, Mr. Moss," Babin said, "last night you inadvertently inserted yourself into a family dispute that…"

"All I did was open my door and somebody cold-cocked me," Jackie interrupted.

"You inserted yourself into a family dispute," Babin continued, "that should remain a family dispute. Once you are gone, the Dawson family believes that they can handle the situation internally."

"What about the townsfolk?" I asked. "They're going to forget this?"

"Buford is like the feudal system in the old country," Babin said. "The serfs do what the landowners say"

I couldn't disagree with his comparison.

"So, The Major shot The Colonel?" I said.

"Maybe The Colonel *did* know he was *shtuping* his wife," Jackie said.

"I didn't say that," Babin replied. "I am sure that whatever might have happened was an accident."

"And, the attempted murder and rape charges?" I asked.

"When you are gone, they will be gone."

Jackie and I exchanged another look of disbelief.

"Major Dawson," Babin said, "has asked me to convey his deepest apologies for what has happened."

"He can stick his apology up his *tuchis*," Jackie said.

I grabbed hold of his arm, and he got the message to shut up.

"Please believe me," Babin said, "in a very few days, this will all just be an unhappy memory."

The BMW rounded a curve. I spotted an olive-green Chevrolet Camaro parked at the side of the road.

"Here we are," Babin said.

The dust covered Camaro had seen better days. The right rear fender had a deep dent in it; the paint had rust spots, and the front bumper was sagging.

"Is this a Hertz rental?" Jackie quipped.

"It will get you to the airport," Babin said, stopping the BMW behind the Camaro.

He got out of the car. "Come, gentlemen," he said. "Let us get your luggage out of the trunk."

Jackie and I climbed out of the back of the BMW. "Why are you doing this?" I asked Babin.

"Major Dawson is a business associate. It is good business to do favors for business associates."

He opened the BMW's trunk. Jackie and I retrieved our suitcases, then walked over to the battered Camaro.

"Does this run?" Jackie asked.

"It runs," Babin smiled.

"Let's get out of here," Jackie said, moving to open the car door.

I put my hand on his arm, and he stopped.

Perhaps my paranoia was the result of seeing too many gangster movies. I turned to Babin. "You start it," I said.

Babin hesitated, then started to chuckle. "You do not trust me, my friend?"

Jackie's eyes widened. "You think there's a bomb in there?" he said, backing up a couple of steps.

"Just start it," I insisted.

"Certainly," Babin said. He walked around to the driver's side of the Chevy and slid behind the wheel.

Jackie and I both backed up a few more steps.

Babin turned on the ignition. The car engine sputtered for a moment, then it caught and began purring like a kitten.

Well, maybe a kitten with a slight "knock."

"See," Babin said, stepping out of the car, leaving the engine running, "no BOOM!"

"Let's get out of here," Jackie said.

We grabbed our suitcases and stowed them in the rear seat of the Chevy.

"You drive," Jackie said.

"Follow this dirt road to the main road," Babin instructed, as I approached the driver's side of the vehicle.

"How far is it?" I asked.

"Less than a kilometer."

He could see that I was no genius at the metric system.

"Much less than a mile," he said.

Jackie was already seated in the passenger seat. "Let's go," he said.

I slid behind the wheel and adjusted the seat.

"I am flying home today," Babin said, as I shifted the Chevy into gear. "So, don't be alarmed if you see me following behind you to the airport."

"You can join us in the V.I.P. lounge," Jackie quipped.

Then, to me again: "Let's go!"

I released the emergency brake. The Chevy lurched forward, and we proceeded down the level dirt road.

CHAPTER NINE

Okay, here's another one of those moments that I didn't actually witness, but was told to me later.

When Angie Benedict left the jailhouse that morning, the street outside of the red brick structure was virtually deserted, except for Donny Olson and his younger brother, Freddy. They were across the street, leaning against the front of the dry goods store, eyeing the jailhouse.

Freddy worked as a part time stock boy in the store. Donny was employed at The Factory on the toilet seat production line. But, everybody in town knew that somewhere up in the wooded hills above Buford, the boys also operated a still.

Angie Benedict didn't like either one of these over-sized, scraggly-bearded roughnecks; the town bullies, always looking for a fight. They'd stroll the street in their unwashed overalls, T-shirts and stained windbreakers, and if someone was in their path, they would brush them out of the way. Most folks, when they saw the brothers coming, just stepped off the sidewalk and let them pass.

And, they got away with it. The sheriff wouldn't touch them.

That was because the Olsons sometimes did questionable odd jobs for and were under the protection of the Dawson family.

Angie Benedict knew all this and more because she was an undercover agent for the F.B.I.

She was the perfect choice for this assignment, since she had been raised in Buford, but departed in her early teens when her parents sent her off to a private school.

Actually, that was a lie; her cover story. She was really from Nashville. Her family was well to do. She did attend a private school, and then earned a law degree at the University of Tennessee. After that, she accepted an invitation to join The Bureau.

And, her *real* name was Angela Goodwin, but I'm going to keep calling her "Angie Benedict" in this account to avoid confusion.

When the Dawson's invented their "doo-hickey" and refused to turn oversight for its manufacture over to the government, the Feds decided that they needed to have eyes and ears in the town of Buford to make sure that this top secret device would not fall into the wrong hands.

Fortunately for their plan, the owner of the Grand Hotel had just passed away and there appeared to be no legal heirs… until, suddenly, a will was found, naming one "Angela Benedict" as sole beneficiary.

Nobody in Buford seemed to know or remember an "Angela Benedict," or that the owners of the Grand even had any offspring, but Abner Whitcomb had driven down the mountain to Little Rock, searched the public records and found both the recorded will and Angela Benedict's birth certificate.

Isn't the Federal Government amazing?

Partly because of her Southern background, Angie Benedict (aka: Goodwin), who had been working routine racketeering cases up to that point, was offered the assignment. She was to assume the new identity, move to Buford, take over management of the Grand and become a part of the community. She would be a "mole," and the assignment might last for years.

This was not a choice undertaking, but Angie Benedict had recently ended a romantic relationship with a fellow agent, and she needed to get away from her New York field office.

Angie Benedict missed "civilization." She missed theatre, good movies and, most of all, conversing with people about more than Clara Sue Morgan's special recipe for apple pie and the fact that Homer Humphrey's prize hog just had another litter.

Without the Book of the Month Club, she would have gone insane years ago.

Truly, after five years in this backward mountain "prison," she was more than ready to move on. And, with what had been happening in Buford during the last twenty-four hours, it looked like she was about to get her opportunity.

Freddy Olson waved at her from across the street. "Hiya, Miz Angie," he said.

Angie Benedict forced a smile and waved back, then walked to the end of the short block and turned the corner.

At the alley, she spotted the BMW parked behind the rear entrance of the jailhouse, then she proceeded past her cream-colored Dodge Coronet, and turned the next corner.

She opened the rear door of the Cadillac limousine and slipped inside.

"They're about to move them," she said to Edward Webster, who was seated behind the wheel. He was still dressed in his chauffeur's uniform.

"Babin's BMW is sitting right behind the jail."

"The Major told me to come back for him in thirty minutes," Edward said, "so I guess he's not goin' with them."

"I spotted the Olson brothers out front," Angie Benedict said. "They're just watching the place."

"That's not good."

Edward Webster, actually, was from Buford and he did leave town when he was a young man. He'd joined the navy and now held the rank of Commander, working in Naval Intelligence. A widower, he'd been planning his retirement when the Buford assignment came up five years ago. Since Buford was his hometown, Edward couldn't disagree that he was the perfect man for the undercover job.

Luckily, though they knew nothing of his military career, the Dawson's remembered him when he was a gangly youth, and they certainly had warm feelings for his grandfather, who had recently passed. When Edward had returned to take care of his grandfather's affairs, they'd offered him the old man's job as the family's chauffeur.

But, his real job, as was Angie Benedict's, was to make sure that the doo-hickey for the RIM-3H5 guided missile program didn't fall into the wrong hands.

I know I keep calling this thing a "doo-hickey," but to this very day, I have absolutely no idea what this "Top Secret" device really was.

"What do you think?" Edward asked Angie Benedict.

"If we don't do something, they'll kill them."

"I know," he said. "Maybe it's time to pull the plug."

"The phone lines are down."

"My radio isn't," Edward said. "I just have to get away from The Major long enough to get to it."

"Then, let's call in the Marines."

"Agreed," Edward said. "But, that's going to take a few hours. In the meantime…"

"In the meantime," Angie Benedict interrupted, "I'm going to see that nothing happens to them."

"You need help?"

"You just make sure that the Marines get here," she said, opening door of the limousine. She headed back around the corner toward the alley.

Now, you might wonder why Angie Benedict might put herself out to save Jackie and me, a pair of virtual strangers.

It turns out that, last night, after the show and I'd gone to bed, Jackie stayed up and played Gin Rummy with Angie

Benedict for almost two hours. She'd blitzed him every game, and she'd found his grumping and growling each time she'd announced, "Gin," to be funny and rather charming. After a while, he'd started making jokes about his lousy hands and started smiling.

She said she hadn't had as much fun since she'd moved to Buford.

Of course, unlike me or Ray Crystal or Barbara, Jackie's former wife, Angie Benedict didn't have to deal with the grumping and growling on a daily basis.

But, that might come later. First, she had to save our asses.

Angie Benedict peered down the alley, just in time to see the BMW drive away. She saw The Major watching it depart, and then step back inside the jailhouse and shut the door.

She hurried over to the Dodge Coronet and slid behind the wheel. As she started the engine, she reached down under the front seat and retrieved the .38 Smith & Wesson Special she kept stowed there. She set it on the seat next to her.

She put her car into gear, and then turned down the alley, heading in the same direction as the BMW.

She would follow at a distance.

10 CHAPTER TEN

I know you're anxious to get back to Jackie and me, but here's just one more of those moments that I didn't actually witness, and was told about later.

The Olson boys were still across the street when The Major stepped out of the jailhouse. He nodded to the pair just as Edward rounded the corner in the Cadillac limousine and pulled up in front of him.

The brothers got the message. They walked down the street to their gray Ford pick-up truck that had seen better days, got inside, and then headed down the hill.

The Major slid into the back seat of the limo. "Take me to the clinic," he ordered.

"Yes, sir, Major," Edward replied. He made a U-turn, then headed the vehicle up the hill toward The Factory.

The clinic was a converted two-bedroom frame house that sat on the hill behind The Factory. It was the closest thing in the town of Buford that resembled a hospital or, in fact, offered any sort of medical aid to the townsfolk. It had four beds, but no doctor. If somebody required major medical attention, they had to travel down the mountain to Little Rock.

Pamela Parkinson, a sixty-two-year old registered nurse, ran the clinic, and she was perfectly capable of dispensing aspirins, treating the flu, stitching up minor wounds and, if necessary, delivering babies.

Pamela was tall. Her body was razor-thin, and folks in Buford sometimes joked that if she stood next to a flagpole in the twilight, you couldn't tell them apart.

The Colonel was currently occupying one of the beds at the clinic, and he would be until the helicopter arrived to take him down to Little Rock. Unfortunately, this morning, the cloud cover on the mountain was low, and that visibility condition was delaying the emergency transport.

The Major didn't know what he was going to do about his older brother. As much as he resented him, Frank was still his brother. He didn't want him dead.

He just wanted him out of his way.

And now, Babin had probably fixed that.

Last night, after the party, The Major had gone down to the hotel to meet with Babin. He told him that, with The Colonel in charge of The Factory, the deal was not going to happen, not for five million, not for twenty.

The man from Prague was not happy with the news.

And then, Frank had showed up. He'd followed his brother to the hotel in order to confront Babin face-to-face. He was going to hammer the final nail into the coffin of the deal himself.

There was no way that Babin or any foreign government was going to get the blueprints for the doo-hickey.

They were in the upstairs hallway of the hotel.

Their angry voices got louder.

The Colonel pulled a revolver from his coat pocket and brandished it at the European.

With scant effort, the military-trained Babin wrestled it from his grip.

Then, the door behind The Colonel opened and a yawing Jackie Moss, attired in T-shirt and shorts, started to step out into the hallway.

"What the…?" is all he said before Babin smashed him across the head with the revolver.

Jackie staggered back two steps and collapsed into his room.

Babin had then pointed the weapon at Frank and fired.

The bullet hit The Colonel in the head. He fell onto the floor, unconscious.

The Major's first instinct was to attack Babin. He had, after all, shot his brother.

But, Babin had pointed the revolver at him, prepared to fire a second round. He said one word: "Think!"

The Major stopped.

He knew what Babin was saying.

If the truth of this shooting ever came to light, all would be lost.

The Feds would invade Buford; take over The Factory. The Major would be charged with treason and, if his brother died, accessory to murder.

Voices emanated from the first floor of the hotel. People had heard the shot and were trying to discern where it had come from.

Babin had moved quickly. He walked into Jackie's room, kneeled by the unconscious man and placed the revolver into his hand.

"He did it," Babin said, rejoining The Major.

The Major was confused. 'Why would he?" he asked.

"Wasn't that The Colonel's daughter...your niece...up in his room this afternoon?"

"I don't know what room she was in." The Major said.

Babin shrugged. "Perhaps your brother heard about it," he said. "Perhaps he came down here tonight to defend his daughter's honor. Perhaps Mr. Moss took his gun away from him."

"Nobody's going to believe that," The Major said.

They heard footsteps. People were starting to come up-stairs.

"Your brother is unconscious," Babin said. "Moss is un-conscious.... You and I are the only witnesses."

And, that was the story that they told Angie Benedict, who was the first person to top the stairs to the second floor, the sheriff and everybody else.

Jackie was arrested. I was arrested.

After we were taken to the jailhouse, Babin and The Major put their heads together to decide how they were going to prevent The Colonel or us from revealing what really had taken place.

"Go grab yourself some breakfast," The Major said to Edward, as the limousine stopped in front of the clinic. "Be back for me in an hour."

"Yes, sir, Major," Edward said.

The Major got out of the car and watched it drive away. "Edward shouldn't be driving at that fast a speed," he thought. "Maybe he's hungry or maybe he just has to get to the bath room."

Eyeing the front of the clinic, The Major lit a cigarette, took a deep drag and pondered the events of the past several hours.

He was uneasy with the plan that Babin had proposed.

He wasn't a murderer. He hadn't shot his brother. He'd never shot anybody.

But, if he didn't go along with the scenario Babin had laid out, he could spend the rest of his life in a Federal prison.

On the other hand, if Babin's plan worked, he'd be off the hook. The deal for the doo-hickey would go through, nobody would be the wiser, and The Major would be a very rich man.

The first thing he had to do was temporarily disable the phone lines that connected Buford with the outside world. That had not been a momentous problem, since the Dawson family owned the local phone company and the exchange was on The Factory property.

As Babin had pointed out, until the situation was "handled," there could be no calls made to the State Police or any Federal Government agencies.

It was also The Major's job to manage his brother…if he lived.

The Colonel was a businessman, and he would understand that, if the Feds got wind of what had happened, that would be the end of everything: The Factory and the Dawson family.

Like Jackie Moss had said, what happened in Buford had to stay in Buford.

At least, The Major hoped his brother would understand that.

Babin's assignment in the scheme was a bit more complex. With the help of the Olson brothers, he had some loose ends to tie up: Jackie and me.

Despite his current career downturn, Jackie was still a well-known public figure. Conceivably, he could appear on television and talk to newspaper reporters about what had happened to him in Buford. He might even make light of his experiences and include jokes about them his nightclub act.

People in the Federal Government watched television, read newspapers and went to nightclubs, so there was no way that Babin or The Major could let that come to pass.

The Major tossed down the cigarette, stepped on the butt, and then walked inside the clinic.

What greeted him took him totally by surprise.

CHAPTER ELEVEN

11

B abin was right.

It was less than a mile before we reached the main road down the mountain.

He must have been following us at some distance, because not once did I see him behind us in the rearview mirror.

I braked when we came to the end of the dirt road; looked both ways, then headed down the mountain.

"Do you remember how to get to the airport?" Jackie asked.

"No. I wasn't doing the driving when we came up here."

"Damn!"

"Don't worry," I said. "We'll find it."

"I just want to get out of this place," he said. "They may hate me in Vegas, but at least they're not trying to lynch me."

"Yet."

Jackie chuckled. "I do the jokes, remember?"

I was beginning to feel myself relaxing slightly, though I was uncomfortable driving down this narrow two-lane road. The clouds were low over the mountain and there was a morning mist. To the left of us was a wall of trees and to the right, a steep drop-off down the mountain that made Mulholland Drive in Los Angeles almost look like a flatland.

"I'm going to miss that Angie Benedict," Jackie said, staring out his window.

"She's a nice lady," I said.

"A class act," Jackie said. "I don't know why she stays in a toilet like Buford."

"She owns the hotel."

"She should sell it. Move to New York…Los Angeles…."

"And, then what?"

"I don't know," Jackie said. "Maybe I could help her find something."

"Jackie," I said, "you've got enough problems of your own right now. You don't need another 'project'."

"I know," he said, continuing to stare out his window. "But, I like her."

A curve in the road was up ahead. I pressed down on the brake pedal, and my foot hit the floor.

"No brakes!" I said.

"No brakes!?!" Jackie repeated.

I turned the wheel to the left; made the curve, but the grade was getting steeper and we were picking up speed.

I pulled the emergency brake.

Nothing.

"What happened to the goddamn brakes!?!" Jackie shouted.

"I don't know!" I shouted back.

Another curve was coming up fast.

"Pull over!" Jackie shouted, his eyes wide, the blood draining from his face.

"Pull over where?" I shouted back. "You want to crash into a tree?"

"Better than going off a cliff!"

I turned the wheel right, then left, successfully negotiating the next curve.

"Good move," Jackie said. "Now, stop this bastard."

"Shut up, Jackie," I said. "Let me concentrate."

"Concentrate!" he said, gripping his seat.

The solid wall of trees continued on our left, and a hundred yards in front of us was another curve.

But, just before that bend on the left side of the road was a turn-out; barely a few yards wide.

"Get down on the floor, Jack," I said, "and brace yourself. I'm going to try something."

"What!?!"

"Get down, damnit!"

Jackie moved his ass down onto the floor.

The turn-out was coming up fast.

I jerked the wheel hard to the left, and the Camaro screeched into a U-turn. For a moment, I thought we might tip over, but we didn't.

Instead, the Camaro barreled deep into the turn-out and sideswiped a couple a trees, shattering both windows on the right side of the car.

At that point, I was tossed against the left door and lost control of the vehicle.

The front bumper caught onto one of the trees.

The car spun half way around and stopped, facing the woodland wall.

The rear end of the Camaro was partially out into the road, but then the vehicle slowly rolled forward a bit and smashed into a tree, popping open the hood.

Steam began escaping from the cracked radiator.

My shoulder hurt from where it hit the door.

I looked over at Jackie. He had a few shards of glass on him, but he wasn't cut.

"Are you okay?" I asked.

"Am I alive?"

"You're alive."

"Then, I guess I'm okay," he said.

"Let's get out of this heap before it explodes."

"Good idea."

The car wasn't on fire or anything like that, but after the past twenty-four hours, who knew what could happen?

I pushed my back against the door, and it popped open. I stepped out of the Camaro and rubbed my shoulder.

Jackie was still stuck on the floor of the passenger's side, and there was broken glass on the seat.

"Hold on," I said, moving around to the other side of the car. "Let me help you."

I glanced at the front of the Camaro and the trickling water from the broken radiator. The thin stream was running down the incline; forming a small pool at the lower edge of the turn-out. Just above that pool was what appeared to be the start of a narrow foot path extending into the dense woods.

"Stop looking at the scenery and get me out of here," Jackie snapped.

I took hold of the passenger door and tried to open it.

It was stuck; probably a result with its encounter with the trees.

"Jack, push your back against it," I said.

Jack pushed. I pulled.

My shoulder ached.

Jack pushed some more, and I pulled some more.

My shoulder ached some more.

Then, I looked through the shattered window and noticed that the door was locked.

Schmuck!

"Jackie," I said, "unlock the door."

"What?"

"Unlock the door!"

He looked at the door, scowled, and then reached up and unlocked it.

I pulled the door open, and Jackie fell out onto his back.

"You okay?" I asked, as I helped him to his feet. I rubbed my shoulder.

"I'm fine," he said through gritted teeth. He brushed some glass shards off his clothes. "What the hell happened?"

"I don't know?"

"You think they drained the brake fluid?"

"Maybe," I said.

"If we were killed in an accident...."

I finished Jackie's sentence. "Nobody outside of Buford would be asking questions about what happened last night."

"Damnit!" Jackie said. "I can just see the headline: 'JACK-IE MOSS KILLED IN AUTO ACCIDENT'.... Even my publicist can't get me that kind of press."

"You don't need to be the next James Dean," I said, rubbing my shoulder.

"What's the matter with your arm?" he asked.

"I bumped it when I got thrown against the car door."

He reached over and felt my shoulder.

"Is it broken?"

"I don't think so. Just bruised."

"It doesn't feel like it's broken," Jackie said.

"Thank you, doctor."

"You're welcome," he said. "I'll send you my bill."

"I'll send you a check."

We both smiled, briefly.

He looked over at the disabled Camaro. "So, now what do we do?"

"I guess we're going to walk down the mountain," I said.

"Maybe we can hitch a ride somewhere."

"Babin!" I said, suddenly remembering the Czech.

"Where the hell is he?" Jackie said.

"He was supposed to be following us."

We looked up the road.

"I don't see him," Jackie said.

"Maybe it's just as well."

"You think he set this up?"

"I don't know," I said. "But, let's get our bags and get out of here."

"I'm for that," Jackie said.

I opened the trunk. We grabbed our suitcases, then turned to start trekking down the mountain.

Just then, a gray Ford pick-up, heading up the mountain, rounded the bend and pulled into the turn-out, blocking our path. A pair of hefty, bewhiskered mountain boys shared the front seat.

Jackie threw a quick look in my direction, then waved at the two scruffy gents. "Hi, guys!" he said.

The driver shut off the engine.

"Careful, Jack," I said. "We don't know who these guys are."

"They were coming up the mountain, not down," he said. "So, they're not coming from Buford."

He turned back to the pick-up. "You fellas want to make a few bucks?"

The two men stepped out of the truck. They were both big sons-of-bitches, dressed in grimy overalls and food stained T-shirts. They looked like they could be brothers, and either one of them would have been perfect casting as "Lenny" in John Steinbeck's *Of Mice and Men*.

The only difference was that Steinbeck's "Lenny" didn't look so mean.

The men stood in front of the truck, half glowering; half looking at us like we were some sort of oddity.

Jackie and I took a couple of steps back.

He threw me a nervous glance, then forced himself to smile at the hillbilly behemoths.

"We'll pay you a hundred dollars to drive us to the airport in Little Rock," he said.

The two men didn't say a word. They looked at each other, then back at us.

Jackie swallowed hard. "How about two hundred?" he said.

The men looked at each other again, but remained silent.

"These guys should manage me," Jackie whispered. "They negotiate better than Ray Crystal."

He turned back to the men. "Three hundred," he said. "And, that's my final offer."

"The driver of the truck turned to his companion. "That's more than The Major's payin' us," he said.

"Oh, shit!" I said.

Jackie blanched. "The Major!?!" he stammered. "He's paying you?"

"Yeah," the driver said. "But he's not payin' us three hundred dollars."

I grabbed Jackie's arm. "Let's go!" I said.

"Go where!?!"

I pointed to the narrow footpath that led into the woods. "Anywhere but here!"

"Wait a minute!" Jackie said. He turned back to the behemoths and forced a weak smile.

"What's The Major paying you to do?" he said.

The driver answered simply, honestly. There was no threat in his tone.

"He's payin' us to make sure your car don't get down the mountain."

"Really?" Jackie said, backing up another step.

"Jackie," I whispered, "Let's go!"

The other behemoth finally spoke. His voice was a bit hoarse. "He said your car was goin' to go over the edge."

"And if it didn't," the driver said, "we had to make sure it did."

"Yes," Jackie said, on a sudden roll, "but did he say we had to be in it?"

The driver looked at his companion. "Did he say that?"

"I don't think so."

"I got an idea," Jackie said.

"Oy!" I said under my breath. I looked over at the narrow path into the woods and tried to figure, if we dropped our luggage, how long it would take us to dash over there.

Jackie pointed to the Camaro. "If you guys push this car over the cliff, then you will have done your job, right?"

The men exchanged a glance, then the driver spoke. "Yeah," he said.

"And The Major will pay you?"

The men nodded.

"Then, we'll pay you again for taking us to the Little Rock airport," Jackie said. "You fellas will come out of this smellin' like a rose."

"A rose?" the driver said.

"Or, whatever kind of flower you grow up here."

The driver looked at his companion. "What do you think?"

"I dunno," the second behemoth said. "That car's pretty heavy."

"An' my back's been hurtin' some," the driver said.

"We'll help you push it," Jackie said.

That narrow foot path was looking better to me every second.

"Why don't we just take the money," the second behemoth said, "toss 'em in the car, and push it over?"

"Yeah," the driver said, "that does sound easier."

Jackie started to panic. "Remember your back," he said. "If you do that, we won't help you push the car."

Our "discussion" was interrupted by the BMW, rounding the bend above us; slowing as it approached the turn-out.

"It's Babin!" I shouted, taking Jackie's arm. "Let's go!"

He didn't resist. We broke for the path into the woods.

Behind us, I heard Babin shouting, "Why are you running?"

"Because we're not schmucks!" Jackie yelled back.

"Get them!" Babin barked at the two behemoths.

Jackie and I reached the path. "Where to?" he shouted. "Just go!"

We leaped the small stream created by the water from the broken radiator, and took a few steps up into the woods. I looked back over my shoulder.

Nobody was following us yet. Babin was eyeing us, and he appeared to be giving more orders to the two behemoths. One of them ran to the cab of the pick-up truck. He retrieved two rifles that were mounted on the roof over the dashboard.

I gave Jackie a shove and we headed up into the forest.

CHAPTER TWELVE

A ngie Benedict had been following Babin in his BMW ever since he'd left the Buford jailhouse with Jackie and me crouched down in the back seat.

She'd kept her distance in the Coronet, travelling a couple of blocks behind the other vehicle, but when it turned down the winding dirt side road, she dropped back a bit, making sure that the forest of trees kept her hidden.

About a mile into the woods, she decided to reconnoiter. She'd parked her car, then weapon in hand and making sure she was hidden by the cottonwoods, crept up the road to see what was ahead.

Peering around the first curve, she spotted the BMW and, a few feet away, the Camaro. Jackie and I were standing to the rear of the BMW, watching Babin as he started the older car.

"See," the Czech said, exiting the vehicle, "no BOOM!"

"Let's get out of here," Jackie said.

We threw our suitcases into the back seat, got into the Chevy and drove off down the road.

Angie Benedict maintained her position behind the trees, observing Babin, as he checked his wristwatch, leaned against the BMW and lit a cigarette.

It appeared that he was in no hurry.

He knew we weren't going to get very far.

He checked his watch again, took one last drag on the cigarette, then stomped it out. He got into his car and, at a leisurely pace, headed down the road after the Chevy.

Angie Benedict hurried back to the Coronet and, also at a leisurely clip, started after him.

Actually, as she told us later, she was surprised that Babin had let us drive off. She had expected that he would try to *execute* us somewhere in the woods, then hide our bodies so that we would never be found.

Execute!

Even after all these years, that word still gives me the willies.

As she passed the spot where the Camaro had been parked, she glanced over and noticed a small puddle on the ground. She stopped her car, got out and studied the puddle. Drops of the liquid trailed off in the direction of the Chevy.

She stuck her finger into the wet patch.

There was no odor to the solution, but it had an oily feel. It was definitely not water.

Brake fluid!

Of course, she realized then, Babin was too clever an operative to let Jackie and me simply disappear. That would spark an investigation.

But, if we were killed in an accident....

Like going off a cliff....

Angie Benedict got back into the Coronet. She headed down the dirt road after the BMW and us.

In fact, she increased her speed.

She reached the main road down the mountain and turned right. She knew that, by now, Edward had, hopefully, dropped off The Major and had called in the cavalry....

That's the Marines, to you.

And, it would only be a matter of hours before they came riding to the rescue.

That was the *good* news.

The *bad* news was that Jackie and I might not be around in a matter of hours.

Again, Angie Benedict pressed down on the gas pedal, looking for any signs of where the Camaro might have taken a plunge over the cliff. The morning mist didn't make her task any easier.

She rounded one bend in the road, and then another.

Nothing.

She was beginning to think that perhaps she'd either taken the wrong road or had missed some sign altogether when she negotiated another curve and, through the haze, spotted the three vehicles in the turn out up ahead.

The BMW.

The Camaro.

The gray Ford pick-up.

The Camaro looked like it had crashed into the trees and the other two vehicles were, more or less, blocking it.

Angie Benedict stopped the Coronet fifty yards up the road from the turn out, and watched.

Babin was there, talking to the Olson boys. He looked angry.

The brothers were both carrying rifles and, after a few moments, they lumbered off and disappeared into the woods.

Babin leaned against the BMW and lit a cigarette.

There was no doubt in Angie Benedict's mind as to what was going on.

They were hunting down Jackie and me.

The one thing she was sure of was that, if they wanted our demise to look like the Camaro had plunged over a cliff, the Olson brothers couldn't shoot us.

Sure, they would still kill us, but there couldn't be any bullet holes in our bodies.

As Jackie would later quip: "Knowing that made me feel so much better."

Angie Benedict proceeded down and across the road. She pulled into the turn out behind the BMW.

She grabbed her weapon and, keeping it concealed behind her back, stepped out of the car.

Babin turned and did a slight double-take when he saw her. "Miss Benedict?" he said. "What are you doing here?"

"I'm on my way into Little Rock to pick up some stuff," she said. "What's going on here?"

"Apparently, there has been an accident," he said, studying her and taking another drag off his cigarette. "I stopped to see if I could render assistance, but nobody was around."

"Apparently."

He tossed down his cigarette and stepped on it.

She pointed to the pick-up. "Doesn't that truck belong to one of the Olson brothers?"

"I don't know the Olson brothers," Babin said. "That truck was here when I arrived."

"So, what are you doing out this way?" she asked, beaming a smile. "You're not running out on your hotel bill, are you?"

Babin forced a chuckle. "Of course not," he said. "I, too, have business in Little Rock. I'll be back before this evening."

He stuck his hand into his right jacket pocket.

"I know," she said. "I was just joshing you."

Keeping her weapon concealed against her right leg and staying on the opposite side of the BMW from Babin, she moved over to get a better look at the Camaro.

"My bags are still in my hotel room," he said.

He grasped hold of the stiletto inside his jacket pocket.

"I wonder what happened here," she said. "What became of the driver?"

"Perhaps he was picked up by a passing vehicle."

"Perhaps."

Babin withdrew the stiletto from his pocket and held it down at his side.

"But then," Angie Benedict continued, looking straight at Babin, "what happened to the Olson brothers?"

The Czech smiled; shrugged his shoulders. "I have no idea."

When she turned back to look at the Camaro, he snapped open the blade to the stiletto.

Angie Benedict heard the snap. She knew what it was, but she didn't react.

She turned back to face Babin. "I wonder if the driver got disoriented and wandered off into the woods."

Babin smiled and shrugged again. "I guess that could have happened," he said, edging toward the front of the BMW.

"Maybe the Olson brothers went looking for him."

"Of course," Babin said, "he could have gone in the other direction and fallen off the edge."

"That could have happened, too," she said. "But then, that wouldn't explain what happened to the Olson brothers."

He was now at the grille of the vehicle, and moving closer.

"You're sure you didn't see anybody?" she said.

"Positive."

"That's strange," she said.

He was at the passenger's side of the grille. "Why is that strange?"

"Because," she said, turning to face him, "when I was coming down the road, I saw you talking to the Olsons, and then they ran off into the woods."

Babin stopped moving. He forced a smile. "You're very observant," he said.

"That's what they teach us in the F.B.I." she said.

The Czech's mouth dropped and he went pale. "F.B.I.?" he gasped.

"F.B.I." She started to bring up her weapon.

Babin raised the stiletto and thrust forward.

CHAPTER THIRTEEN

Jackie and I were deep into the woods when we heard the shot.

It sounded like it came from back where we left the Camaro.

"What the hell was that?" he said.

"I dunno," I said. "It sounds far away. I don't think they're shooting at us."

"Then, who are they shooting at?" He slapped a gnat off his neck.

We continued up the narrow dirt path that wound through the dense array of pines and cottonwoods.

I'm no botanist, so I'm just assuming they were pines and cotton-woods.

We rounded another bend, and then I stopped. "Wait a minute," I said. "this is no good."

"Why is it no good?" Jackie said.

"We don't know where the hell we're going."

"We're following this path."

"But, we don't know where it leads," I said.

"Probably to some moonshiner's cabin."

"You think a moonshiner is going to welcome us with open arms? I've seen enough movies to know what they do with Revenue Men up here."

"We can't go back" Jackie said. There's two or three guys down there, and they have guns."

"And, they're probably following us."

"What do you suggest?"

"I'm not sure," I said, shrugging my shoulders. "I wasn't a Boy Scout, and I've never even been camping."

"I wasn't a Boy Scout either," Jackie said. "I wasn't a Cub Scout and I wasn't a Camp Fire Girl. But, we both went through basic training in the Army."

"Almost thirty years ago."

"What do you think we should do?" he insisted.

"This path is just taking us further up into the mountains…."

"Agreed."

"I think we should leave the path, double back a bit and head in the general direction of the main road that runs down the mountain."

Jackie looked at me liked I'd lost my mind. "Are you meshugge?" he said. "What main road? We're surrounded by trees!"

"That's why we double back," I said. "At some point we should be parallel to the road and we can follow it down the mountain."

"All the way to Little Rock?"

"No," I said, "there was that gas station we stopped at. They had a phone there."

Jackie mulled my idea. "We're going to leave the path?" he said.

"I think we have to."

He looked down at his clothes. "Well, my new tux is ruined anyway," he said, slapping a gnat off his face. "The bugs are eating me alive. What else have I got to lose?"

"You want me to answer that?" I asked.

He slapped another gnat.

"Okay, let's go," I said. I stepped off the path and made my way past the first couple of trees.

Jackie followed. "You think there're wild animals in here?" he asked.

"Probably."

"Lions and tigers and bears, oh my!"

"Probably just bears," I chuckled, as I endeavored to get my bearings.

"And, rabbits?"

"I guess."

"Tell me about the rabbits, George," he said. "Please tell me about the rabbits."

"Enough with the John Steinbeck already," I said. "I'm trying to concentrate."

"Would you rather I scream?" he said. "Talking keeps me calm."

"And, if those people are following us, they can hear you talking."

He quickly ran his finger across his mouth, indicating that his lips were sealed.

We continued to maneuver our way through the trees, heading away from the dirt trail and back in the direction of the main road.

I heard voices behind us. I motioned to Jackie and we both ducked down behind a tree.

Back on the path, the two behemoths were tramping up the mountain. They were both carrying rifles, but they didn't appear to see us.

"The two Lennies," Jackie whispered, referring again to Steinbeck's *Of Mice and Men*.

I zipped my finger across my lips and he shut up.

"You really think they're headin' up to Zeke Medford's?" we heard the first behemoth say.

"Looks like it," the other behemoth answered.

"What if they find his still?"

"Told you it was moonshiners," Jackie whispered.

I glowered at him and he shut up.

"Zeke'll shoot 'em," the first behemoth said.

"The foreigner back there said we shouldn't shoot 'em."

"He didn't tell Zeke that."

The two behemoths disappeared into the trees and their voices trailed off.

"I got an idea," Jackie whispered.

"What?"

"They're going up the mountain. Why don't we go back down the trail, and...."

I interrupted him. "Because Babin is down there," I said. "And, he might have a gun."

Jackie deflated. "Yeah, he probably does," he said.

"Let's stick to the plan."

"Lead on, MacDuff," Jackie said with a nod.

"We'll go this way," I said, moving through the foliage. "Maybe we can get to a spot where we can see the main road."

"And, then what?"

"Then, we find a way to get down to it."

Jackie slapped another gnat off his face, and we trudged on.

Thirty minutes later we were still surrounded by trees, no main road was in sight, gnats were still feasting on Jackie's neck and face like it was a Passover feast (*I guess they didn't like me*) and I had no idea where the hell we were.

We were lost.

"I thought you knew what you were doing," Jackie scowled.

"I'm sorry," I said. "I was trying to gage our position by the Sun.

"What Sun?" Jackie said, pointing upward. "The trees are so thick you can hardly see the sky."

"Okay," I said. "I'm sorry. I screwed up."

Jackie's gaze moved to just beyond my right shoulder. I didn't like the look in his eyes.

"What do you want to do?" I said. I turned to see where he was gaping at.

It was a black bear, standing in the woods about twenty feet away from us.

It appeared to be a young bear, medium-sized; not threatening, just curious as to the two strange intruders in his forest.

"I think we should...*RUN*," Jackie said. He started to move away.

I grabbed his arm. "No," I said, "don't run. He'll chase us."

"How do you know that?"

"I read it in a book."

"The same book that told you how to find your way out of the woods?"

I didn't answer him. I just watched the bear.

"So, what are we supposed to do?" Jackie said, a bit of panic seeping into his voice. "Wait here until he decides to eat us?"

"If we run, we're prey."

"I am praying," Jackie said.

The bear just stood there, continuing to look at us.

Jackie waved at the animal. "Nice bear," he said.

The bear emitted a mild, not too menacing growl, then continued to stare at us.

"Is he saying 'hello'?" Jackie asked.

"Let's back up," I suggested. "Real slow."

We moved away from the bear, one step at a time.

The bear moved toward us, one step at a time.

We stopped.

The bear stopped.

We took another step backward.

The bear took a step.

"What is he? A stray?" Jackie said. "You think he wants us to take him home and adopt him.?'"

The bear growled again. He took another step forward.

I reached down and picked up a large rock.

"What are you going to do?" Jackie asked.

"Strike him out, I hope." I extended my arm back to throw the rock at the bear.

It's a good thing I'm right handed, because my left shoulder still ached.

"Don't!" Jackie said. "He'll get mad."

"Get ready to take off," I said.

Jackie took a step or two away from me. His heel hit a protruding tree root. He stumbled backward and landed on his tuchis.

Gnats swarmed up from the disturbed foliage. They renewed their meal on Jackie's neck and face. Slapping the Kamikaze bugs away, he regained his footing.

The bear growled again. He kept advancing toward us.

"You okay?" I said.

"Yes," Jackie said. "Throw the damn thing already!"

"Fetch!" I yelled, throwing the rock as hard as I could.

I hit the bear right on the snout. It cried out in pain.

"Run!" I shouted, turning tail and taking my own advice.

Neither Jackie nor I looked back.

CHAPTER FOURTEEN

Angie Benedict ripped Babin's white shirt into strips, wadded one up and pressed it against his bullet wound.

The door of the BMW was open. He was sitting on the driver's side; bare chested, his legs outside the vehicle and his right hand cuffed to the steering wheel.

"You're very lucky," Angie Benedict said. "The bullet went right through. You're not bleeding too badly."

The Czech winced as she secured the wadded strip to his shoulder with a second piece of his shirt. "I don't feel lucky," he said. "That was a silk shirt."

She smiled at his attempt at humor, but she didn't like his pallor. She draped his suit jacket over his shoulders to help keep him warm. "Sorry, I don't have a blanket," she said.

He had come at her with a stiletto, and she only had time to fire the weapon in her hand from the hip.

The slug had hit his left shoulder. Had she had another second to react, he would be dead.

He'd stumbled backward, falling over the front bumper of the BMW and onto the ground. She'd kicked the stiletto out of his right hand, then pinned that hand to the ground with her foot.

"Are we done?" she'd asked.

He'd nodded, then grimaced from the pain.

She'd done a quick pat-down, then stepped back and pointed her weapon at him. "Get up!" she'd ordered. "Face the car."

Using the bumper of the BMW for leverage, Babin pushed himself up with his right hand and leaned against the vehicle. Angie Benedict did another frisk. She tossed his wallet, passport, comb and a bulging money clip onto the hood of the car. There were no other weapons.

After she'd moved him over to the front seat of the BMW and secured him to the steering wheel, she'd gone into her Clara Barton mode.

And, for those of you who flunked history in high school, Clara Barton was a nurse during the Civil War who founded the American Red Cross.

"Where are Jackie Moss and his friend?" she asked Babin, as she tightened the makeshift bandage to his shoulder.

"I don't know."

"Of course, you know," she said. "I followed you from the jail. I saw them take that Camaro that's crashed over there, and I saw you follow them after that."

"You're very.... How do they say it in America? .... on the ball."

"Look, Mr. Babin," Angie Benedict said. "We already have you for espionage and for the attempted murder of a Federal agent. Me! Now,..."

"Excuse me," Babin interrupted. "No illegal transactions have taken place. No secret documents have exchanged hands. And, as far as this altercation between us is concerned: I was using my knife to clean under my fingernails. I tripped in your direction. You panicked and shot me. It was an unfortunate misunderstanding.

"Now, if you will please get me to a doctor, so that my wound can be tended to properly."

Angie Benedict squatted next to him, suppressing a smile. "Mr. Babin," she said, "the Bureau has been aware of your clandestine activities for months. We haven't arrested you before because we wanted to see where you would lead us. And, you led us to the Dawson family.

"The truth is that you are currently on the hook for espionage, successful or not, and assault. You're going to prison. Not a nice prison. But, chances are that, sometime in the future, your side is going to have one of our people and they're going to want to trade for you."

Babin smiled, but didn't speak.

"Jackie Moss is a very famous man," Angie Benedict continued. "If anything happened to him and you were a part of it, I doubt very much if that trade would ever take place."

"What is that magic phrase you have in this country?" Babin asked. "Oh, yes! I want a lawyer."

Angie Benedict stood up. "Unfortunately, Mr. Babin...," she started to say.

"You may call me 'Paul'."

"Unfortunately, Paul," she said, "there's no phone out here and I'm not taking you anywhere until I find Jackie Moss."

"Pity," Babin said with another grimace.

Her prisoner secured, Angie Benedict walked over to examine the Camaro. She peered inside. There was broken glass, but no blood, which was a good thing.

She moved over to the trees and immediately spotted the dirt path that went into the forest. "Oh, Christ," she said aloud, debating whether she should leave Babin where he was and go venturing after us. There were miles and miles of mountains and dense woodlands, and she knew that we could be anywhere.

Her thought process was interrupted by the sound of a car.

The Dawson's Cadillac limousine pulled into the turn-out.

Edward was behind the wheel and he was alone.

She hurried over to him. "How did you know we were here?" she asked, as he stepped out of the car.

"I didn't," he said. "I just figured that Babin was going to stage some sort of accident, so I was just following the road down the mountain until I came across it."

"Did you get through to the base?"

Edward nodded. "They're sending a squad of Marines," he said. "They'll be here in two or three hours.

"What about The Major?" she asked.

"I dropped him at the clinic."

"Isn't he going to miss you?"

"If he does, he'll fire me before I arrest him. He's not going anywhere."

He looked about. "Where're Moss and his friend?"

She pointed to the dirt path. "I think they ran up into the mountains there," she said. "And the Olson Brothers are chasing them."

"If they're in there, we're going to need more than a squad."

He spotted Babin, sitting in the front seat of the BMW. "What happened here?" he asked, walking over to the wounded man.

Angie Benedict explained how her prisoner came to be hurt. "He's asked for a lawyer," she said.

"I'd ask for one, too, sir," he said to Babin.

"I presume you are not really a chauffeur," Babin said.

"Navy Intelligence."

"Of course," Babin said. "But, the truth is that, even if I wanted to help you, I couldn't. I am a stranger to these mountains. I know nothing about these woods."

Edward and Angie Benedict looked at each other. They knew he was telling the truth.

CHAPTER FIFTEEN

Jackie and I ran.

We both tripped over shrubs or roots a couple of times, but we picked ourselves up and kept going.

We jumped across a small stream.

Actually, I jumped. Jackie slipped on a rock and fell into the water.

I helped him up, and we continued running.

Actually, I ran. He sloshed.

We darted around more tree trunks, ducked under more low hanging branches, until we were both winded.

"Is he still chasing us?" Jackie yelled.

I stopped; leaned against a tree trunk to catch my breath. "I don't know," I wheezed.

Jackie halted next to me. He grasped the tree. "Well, look!" he panted.

I took another deep breath, then peered around the tree.

No bear.

Just trees, foliage and the stream behind us.

I listened.

No sounds of a bear.

Just a couple of birds twittering or singing…or whatever birds do.

"I think we lost him," I said.

"Good," Jackie said, sitting down onto the ground. "'Cause I don't think I could run another two feet."

I crashed next to him and while both of us were regaining our wind, I surveyed our surroundings.

Trees.

More trees.

Virtually no sky, and certainly no Sun.

With all our zigging and zagging while running from the bear, not only were we lost, but I no longer had a sense of direction.

"Jackie," I said, "I don't know where we are."

"Well," he said, "we're sure as hell not in Philadelphia."

I didn't answer.

"What do you mean, you 'don't know where we are'?"

"I mean, we're *really* lost," I said. "Back there, before the bear, we probably could have backtracked to the trail. But, now, we've run so far and in so many different directions..."

"Oy!" Jackie said.

"'Oy vay' is more like it."

"Where's Davy Crockett when you need him?"

"He died at The Alamo."

"And, we're going to die in the Ozarks. We'll go to Hillbilly Heaven. You think they have a rabbi up there?"

That's what I loved about Jackie. Even in the bleakest of moments, he could make me smile.

"I doubt it," I said.

"Then, how can we go there?" Jackie said, getting to his feet. "I'll bet they don't even have a decent delicatessen."

I started to laugh. "Probably not," I said.

"What would death be like without lox, bagels and cream cheese?"

"Miserable."

"Get up!" he ordered. "We're going to die in Los Angeles!"

I stood up. "Well, that's something to look forward to," I said.

"What's that over there?" he said, pointing between the trees to a spot about a hundred yards away.

"Looks like the top of a hill."

"So, let's schlep up that hill and see what's on the other side," he said. "We might discover...."

"What?" I said, following him up the mild incline.

"The Pacific Ocean."

"I don't think we've run that far."

"How about a river?"

"I'll settle for a pond."

"David, boychik," Jackie said, "how many times do I have to tell you? Think big!"

We reached the top of the hill and we did discover something.

Not The Pacific Ocean, a river or even a pond.

It was a large circular clearing, right in the middle of the woodlands.

And, in the center of that clearing was a small log cabin with a stone chimney, a barn, and a corral with a gray horse standing inside.

Best of all, behind this farm or ranch or whatever it was, there was a road running over the next hill into (*and, hopefully out of*) the forest.

"What did I tell you?" Jackie beamed. "Mecca!"

He started to move out into the clearing.

I grabbed his arm. "Wait a minute," I said. "We don't know who lives here."

"Probably Ma and Pa Kettle," Jackie said. "Or, maybe even Li'l Abner.... What difference? It's civilization...*light*."

"It could be moonshiners," I said, "and they don't like strangers."

Jackie pointed back into the forest. "Boychik," he said, "we may be lost, but I do know that that dirt path we were following was way back there and it went up the mountain in the opposite direction. That's where the two Lennies said the moonshiner was."

"In these hills, there's got to be more than one moonshiner."

Jackie shook his head. "The people here are probably plain simple folk" he said. "They don't even have a TV antenna, so they probably never even heard of me."

"If that's humanly possible."

"Ha! Ha!" he said. "I wonder if they have a phone."

"I don't see any electric or telephone lines," I said.

"Don't see no car or truck either."

"So, let's just take it slow."

"Slow as mud," Jackie said, half raising his hands and moving into the clearing. "Just in case you're right."

I raised my hands and followed him.

We reached the corral, and Jackie called out to the cabin: "Hello! Anybody home?"

The gray horse walked over to the corral fence and looked at us.

"Fuller Brush Man!" Jackie called.

The horse snorted.

"How you doin'?" Jackie said to the animal.

The horse snorted again.

"Hey, he's a stallion," Jackie commented. "Well endowed, but not Jewish."

"Maybe's nobody's home," I said.

Jackie strolled over; knocked on the cabin door.

No response.

"They could be in the barn," Jackie said, walking in that direction. I tagged along.

The horse seemed agitated. Maybe he didn't like strangers. He started walking about in the corral; rearing up a bit.

Jackie opened the barn door and we were met with a distinctive odor.

"Oh, my God!" I said. "Let's get out of here."

Inside the barn, there was an old banged-up, weather-beaten blue pick-up truck with what looked like brand new tires. There were fifteen or twenty full-sized black Hefty-type garbage bags in the truck's bed. We didn't have to open any of the fully stuffed sacks to know what was in them. The smell was unmistakable.

Weed!

Whoever owned this place was a marijuana grower.

And, considering the quantity of the stash, this guy was definitely not growing it for his own personal use.

"We might have been better off with the moonshiner," Jackie said, then: "You think the keys are inside the truck.?"

"We're *not* stealing a truck?"

"We'll just borrow it."

"And what are you going to tell the cops if we get stopped carrying that load?"

He saw my point. "Gee, officer," he said, "I had no idea…."

Jackie started to shut the barn door, then: "Wanna take a sample?" he said, a gleam in his eye. "It might be good pot."

"Just shut the door."

He shut the door.

The horse whinnied.

"Let's get out of here," I said.

"It would be nice to get something to eat or drink before we go," Jackie said. Maybe there's something inside the house." He started toward the cabin.

"We can't take the people's food," I said.

Jackie kept walking. "I'll leave them a few bucks," he said. "Besides, they're probably so wasted they won't even miss it."

He turned back and looked at the stallion. "Maybe we should borrow the horse," he said.

"No!" I said.

"Who are you?" Jackie growled. "Mr. Goodie Two Shoes all of a sudden?" He went into his mimicking voice. "Can't steal the truck! Can't take the pot! Can't take the food! Can't borrow the horse!"

"I'm your conscience, wooden head. I'm Jiminy Cricket to your Pinocchio."

"I just want us to ride the damn horse out of the mountains," Jackie said. "It would sure as hell be better than walking."

"What are you talking about?" I said. "You've never ridden a horse. And, the only time I've been on one was when I was a kid at a pony ride."

"Of course, I've ridden on a horse," Jackie insisted. Don't you remember that episode of *Rawhide* I did?"

"I stand corrected," I said, attempting to suppress a smile.

"Why are you smiling?"

"I'm trying not to," I said, then started to laugh.

"What!?!"

"Jackie," I said, "you may have sat on the horse and ridden it a bit around the set, but you couldn't mount it. It took two wranglers, off camera, to get you on the damn animal."

"Well, I looked good on the show."

"You looked terrific," I said. "Now, let's go."

Jackie continued over to the cabin door. "Not until we get some food," he said.

There was a loud blast behind us.

Jackie jumped. I thought I was going to have a coronary.

The horse whinnied, raised up on his hind legs and continued to anxiously trot around the corral.

Jackie and I both froze and looked in the direction of the discharge.

Over by the road that led back into the forest was a man holding a smoking shotgun that had just been fired up into the air.

The guy appeared to be in his early forties and might best be described as an "aging hippie." He was a dirty blond, with long stringy hair and a scruffy beard; fashionably dressed for the Ozarks in a soiled T-shirt and jeans.

There was that glazed-over look in his eyes common to people who have smoked too many joints. In fact, aside from the shotgun and a machete strapped to his side, he carried a full Hefty-type garbage bag, which I have no doubt was part of his latest harvest.

"What're you doing here, man?" the guy said.

Neither Jackie or I responded.

"What're you doin' on my land?"

Jackie swallowed hard. "It's a long story," he said finally.

The guy looked over at the corral. "You stealin' my horse, man?"

"No," Jackie said. "We're just...."

The guy dropped the garbage bag and cradled the shotgun in his arms. "Nobody steals my horse," he said.

"I wouldn't steal your horse," Jackie said.

"He can't even mount a horse," I interjected.

"I can't," Jackie said. "Honest."

The guy didn't say anything. He just kept the shotgun pointed in our direction.

"Jackie forced a smile at the guy. "I'm Jackie Moss," he said.

"I'm Stanley Cody," the guy said. "So, what?"

"Any relation to Buffalo Bill?"

"No!"

"I'm a television and movie star," Jackie said.

"I don't go to no movies," Cody said. "Don't have no television neither."

"I do comedy," Jackie said.

"You ain't very funny." He stared at Jackie for several seconds, then: "Were you in *Easy Rider?*"

"No," Jackie said, "I...."

"*Billy Jack?*"

"No."

"Then, I ain't seen you. Movies suck."

"Mr. Cody," I said, "we're in trouble."

"That's right," he said. "Why you tryin' to steal my horse, man?"

"We weren't trying to steal your horse," Jackie insisted.

"He's a smart 'ol horse," Cody said. "Had him fer near six years."

Jackie decided to try a different approach. "What's his name?" he asked.

"Horse. We play checkers together."

"Jackie and I exchanged a worrisome glance. "Follow the yellow brick road," he whispered.

He looked back at Cody. "Who wins?" he asked.

"Sometimes he does. Sometimes I do." He scowled. "Hey," he said, "you makin' fun of me?"

"No," Jackie said, holding up both hands. "Just trying to be friendly."

Cody eyed us suspiciously and gripped his shotgun. "Are you up here to rip off my crop?" he demanded.

Jackie feigned innocence. "What crop?" he said.

"You know what crop!"

Jackie looked at me and shrugged his shoulders.

I played along. "We don't know what you're talking about, mister," I said. "We just went hiking and got lost in the woods."

"Yeah," Jackie added, "we threw down bread crumbs to find our way back, but the birds ate them."

"You're lyin'" Cody said, pulling back the hammer on his weapon. "You're trying to steal my weed!"

"What weeds?" Jackie said. "I got enough weeds in my lawn back home."

I cringed at that one.

"Then, you're the law!" Cody said. He started toward us.

"No!" Jackie shouted.

"We're escaped convicts!" I shouted, blurting out the first idea that came to mind.

Jackie did a double-take in my direction, then picked up on the fable. "Yeah," he said, "we're bank robbers."

Cody stopped. "Like Bonnie and Clyde?" he asked.

"More like Clyde and Clyde," Jackie said.

Cody lowered the shotgun and eyed us for another few seconds. "Thought you said you were a movie star," he said.

"I was," Jackie said. "I was researching one of my roles, and it kinda got out of hand."

Cody pondered that, then: "What prison did you say you escaped from?"

"Alcatraz!" Jackie said, before I could respond.

Now, I knew we were in deep shit. I looked at Jackie, and saw that he knew we were in deep shit, too.

"Alcatraz?" Cody said. "Ain't that in California?"

"I don't know." Jackie said with a gulp. "Is it?"

"If you escaped from Alcatraz," Cody said. "What're you doin' up here in the Ozarks?"

"Hiding out," Jackie said.

My gaze caught some movement in the wall of trees behind Cody.

Emerging from the woods were the two behemoths who had been tracking us. They were both still carrying their rifles.

Cody raised the shotgun again. "I don't believe you," Cody said. "I think you're the law."

"No!" I said. "We're not the law." I pointed toward the two behemoths. "But, they are!"

Cody turned, spotted the pair of Lennies and fired his shotgun.

The behemoths ducked.

The shotgun load went wild.

The horse raised up again, whinnied, then raced and leaped out of the corral. He took off around the barn.

"Horse!" Cody shouted. "You come back here!"

The animal had the right idea. I grabbed Jackie's arm, and we ducked behind the log cabin.

"Stan!" one of the behemoths called out, keeping his head down. "Is that you?"

"Of course, it's me," Cody shouted back. "Who are you?"

"Freddy and Donny Olson," one of them called back.

"You here to steal my weed?" Cody shouted.

"No!" the behemoth said. "We're after those two guys you're with."

"What do ya want them fer?"

"Don't know. The Major and his foreigner friend wants 'em. Sent us to make sure they don't leave the mountain."

Jackie and I didn't need to hear any more. With the cabin blocking Cody and the Olsons from seeing us, we started sprinting toward the road that led into the woods.

We didn't get very far.

The gray horse suddenly galloped out from behind the barn and blocked our way. He whinnied and reared up on his hind legs, challenging us to try to get by him.

"Nice horse," Jackie said.

The horse snorted; pawed its hoof on the ground. It looked like it was ready to fight.

"What do we do?" Jackie said.

On the other side of the cabin, I heard Cody shout, "Where'd they go?"

"You run one way around him and I'll run the other," I said to Jackie. "Maybe it'll confuse him."

Jackie broke to the left. I broke to the right. We both headed toward the road.

The horse went after Jackie; quickly caught up to him and butted him with his head.

Jackie went sprawling.

The horse just stood there; pawing its hoof and watching him.

"Jesus, horse," Jackie said, sitting up and looking at the steed, "what did I ever do to you?"

The horse snorted.

"Get!" I yelled at the beast, as I rushed over to help Jackie.

The horse pranced away toward the barn.

I helped Jackie to his feet.

The horse eyed us, then began to trot back in our direction.

"Come on! Let's go," I said. We started back toward the road.

The horse caught up to us, hindering our way again. It reared up on its hind legs and whinnied.

"I told ya he was a smart ol' horse," Cody called to us, as he emerged from the other side of the log cabin. The Olson boys were right behind him. All three had their weapons at the ready.

"I got 'im trained better than a huntin' dog." Cody said.

Jackie and I both raised out hands.

"Don't forget," Jackie said to the Olsons. "Babin told you not to shoot us."

"He didn't tell me that," Cody said. He raised his shotgun and pointed it at us.

"Hold on!" one of the brothers said to Cody. "He's right. We ain't supposed to shoot 'em."

"Yeah," the other brother concurred. "They're supposed to be in a car accident. Go off a cliff."

"See!" Jackie said with an uncertain note of triumph.

"But, that don't mean we can't beat the holy shit outta them."

"Hey," I said, stepping back a step. Jackie did likewise. "If you beat us up; knock us out, you're going to have to schlep us all the way back down to the car. You want to do that?"

The three men looked at each other a bit befuddled. "Schlep?" one of them asked.

"You're going to have to *carry* us."

"And we're both real heavy." Jackie added. "Remember your back."

Cody and the two behemoths conferred for a moment, then one of the Olson brothers, turned to us. "You gonna be good? Not give us any trouble?"

"We'll be perfect gentlemen," Jackie said. Then, he whispered to me: "When we get back in the woods," we make a run for it."

"Run where?" I whispered back.

"I don't know," Jackie said. "We'll improvise."

Our captors motioned for us to move forward. We obeyed. They fell in behind us, and the horse fell in behind them.

We marched around the log cabin and headed toward the forest from which we'd emerged earlier.

Midway to the trees, Jackie got an inspiration. He stopped unexpectedly; turned to face the three men. "Would you guys be interested in a business proposition?"

"Business proposition?" the smarter of the Olson brothers said.

Actually, I don't know which one was the smarter brother. They were both a few sandwiches shy of a picnic basket. I'm just going to call them smarter and dumber to distinguish them.

"A way to make a lot of money," Jackie said. "The Major is payin' you bubkes to do this."

"Bubkes?"

"Two or three hundred bucks," Jackie said. "That's nothing to what you can make off of my deal."

"Yeah?" the dumber brother said.

"How much can we make?" the smarter one asked.

"Thousands," Jackie said. He was on another roll. He turned to Cody. "I'll bet you sell your crop in Little Rock."

"What's it to you?" Cody glowered at him.

"And, whoever buys it, pays you bubkes, too. Right?"

"They sure as hell pay me more than two or three hundred dollars."

"Jackie," I whispered, "They don't understand Yiddish up here."

"Obviously," he said. Then, to Cody: "They pay you next to nothing; shit."

"They say they got 'distribution expenses', Cody said. "They're just the 'middle men'."

"They're lying to you, my friend," Jackie continued. "Do you grow good stuff?"

"The best in the Ozarks."

The Olson brothers nodded in agreement.

"Great!" Jackie said. "Now, I don't smoke the stuff myself, but I know a hell of a lot of people in Hollywood and New York that do. I can put you in touch with those people and you can sell to them direct.

"You can?" Cody said. "Movie stars?"

"You name 'em. I got 'em."

"Dennis Hopper?" Cody asked. "He was in *Easy Rider*."

Jackie nodded. "He might be your best customer."

Cody seemed to like that idea.

"You'll make so much money that you could move to Beverly Hills," Jackie persisted. "Be like *The Beverly Hillbillies*."

"Who?"

"He doesn't have a television," I reminded Jackie.

"What about us?" the smarter Olson brother asked. "How do we get ours?"

"This will be a huge operation," Jackie said. "Cody'll need a lot of help. You could both be vice presidents."

"Vice presidents?" the dumber brother beamed.

Jackie turned to me. "You think these boys would make good vice presidents. Dave?"

"Anyone would be better than what we have now," I said with a poker face.

"What do you think?" Jackie asked the three men. "Is it a deal?"

"I dunno," the smarter brother said. "The Major'll be pretty sore if we don't do what he paid us fer."

"Screw The Major!" Jackie said.

"Oh, he wouldn't like that," the dumber brother said. "He don't do that kinda thing."

I bit my lower lip, so that I wouldn't smile.

"If we let you go; how do we know you'll do what you say?" Cody asked.

That one stumped Jackie for a moment.

"There's a gas station about halfway down the mountain," I said. "They've got a telephone."

"We know it," the smarter brother said.

"You take us there. We'll call our people in Los Angeles and you can make your deal right over the phone."

"Cody and the brothers looked at each other. "We can do that," Cody said.

"But," I added, "nothing beyond that is going to happen, until we're out of here; back home in Los Angeles."

"Oh, no!" Cody said, raising the shotgun again. "You're stayin' right here with me 'til I get paid fer my crop."

"Yeah!" both brothers said in unison.

"Think we're just dumb mountain folk?' Cody said.

"But, it could take two or three weeks to complete the deal," I said. "Maybe longer."

"Then, it takes two or three weeks, maybe longer," Cody said.

"Yeah!" the brothers said in unison.

"You really like our company that much?" Jackie quipped.

He looked at me. I looked at him. Neither one of us had a clue as to what we should do next.

The horse decided for us.

Suddenly, it whinnied, reared up and, appearing quite agitated, ran off. All of us watched the animal disappear behind the barn.

"What the hell…?" Cody said.

"What spooked him?" the smarter brother said.

I looked over at the trees, and I saw what had frightened the horse.

It was the black bear. It was standing at the edge of the forest, watching us.

Like the two behemoth brothers, I guess it had tracked us here.

Jackie and our three captors, apparently, saw the young beast at the same moment, because they all jumped with a start.

"Jesus!" Cody exclaimed.

The bear growled, but then continued to stare at us in a non-threatening manner.

I wondered if it was trying to be friendly; have a conversation.

Rifles raised, the two brothers pushed their way in front of us and aimed at the bear.

Jackie and I backed up, so that we were behind our three captors. "Don't shoot!" Jackie said. "That's my dog, Spot."

"That's not a dog!" the smarter Olson said. "It's a bear."

"His name is 'Spot'?" the other brother asked.

The smarter brother fired his weapon.

The slug missed, hitting the ground about a foot away from the creature.

The bear turned tail and ran back into the woods.

The two brothers started after him.

Cody stood his ground, watching them.

I was behind him and his back was to me.

I got an insane idea; one I hope that I never have again in my life.

I looked at Jackie. He looked at me. Then, I closed my fist; hauled off and hit Cody right on the side of his head.

My hand hurt like hell, but Cody went down and dropped the shotgun.

While I was holding my painful, battered fist, Jackie rushed in and scooped up the weapon.

Cody was dazed, but he was conscious. He started to clamber to his feet.

The Olson brothers had reached the tree line. The bear had vanished into the forest. They turned around and saw what was happening.

"Hey!" the smarter brother shouted, heading back in our direction.

I grabbed Cody with my good hand and pulled him to his feet. Holding him as a shield between us and the Olsons, Jackie and I started to back toward the barn.

"Where are we goin'?" Jackie asked. He kept the shotgun pointed at the brothers, who were continuing to advance in our direction.

"We'll take the truck." I said.

"Horse!" Cody called out.

The horse came running around the side of the barn. It stopped just behind us, whinnied and raised up on its hind legs. The animal was not going to let us pass.

"You ain't takin' my truck," Cody said.

The Olson behemoths kept moving toward us. They raised their rifles.

Jackie raised the shotgun.

The horse whinnied.

It was what we used to call a Mexican standoff.

Then, we heard the sound.

We all looked up and saw it.

16 CHAPTER SIXTEEN

The Major had already had a rotten day, and it had just become worse.

He'd walked into the clinic's waiting area which, when the structure had served as a residence, had been the living room. Once stark white in color, the room's dim walls and linoleum floor now showed signs of age and occasional stains from human fluids that no amount of scrubbing or disinfectant could ever fully remove.

With the exception of The General, the entire Dawson family was present, sitting on the slightly frayed upholstered sofa and chairs that rimmed the room. The Colonel's wife and daughter, Arlene and Billie Jo, occupied the sofa, while The Major's family, Violet and Billy Jr., sat in chairs on the opposite side of the space.

Nobody appeared to be interacting with each other. Their eye make-up somewhat smeared, the three women looked as if they'd been weeping. Yet, everyone just sat there, dour expressions on their faces; all presumably lost in their own thoughts.

The Major feared the worst.

Violet was the first one to notice him. She stood up, strode over to her husband and slapped him hard across the face. "You son-of-a-bitch!" she shouted, and then she spit into his eye.

The Major staggered back a step. "What the...?"

"Stop!" Arlene called out from her place on the sofa. She began to sob again.

Billie Jo and Billy Jr. just glowered at him.

"You slept with that tramp?" Violet yelled, indicating The Colonel's wife.

The Major noticed a bruise on the side of Arlene's chin.

"My mama's not a tramp," Billie Jo insisted.

"She is if she slept with my Daddy," Billy Jr. said. He turned to his father. "Did she sleep with you, Daddy?"

The Major didn't know how to respond. He wiped the spittle from his face with his handkerchief, looked at his family, and then stammered, "What...whatever gave you that idea?"

Violet pointed once more to Arlene. "She did!"

The Major blanched.

"And then, I hit her."

Arlene's weeping increased a couple of decibels into a low wail.

Billy Jr. leaned forward. "Did she sleep with you, Daddy?" he asked, a bit more lasciviously this time.

"Oh, shut up!" The Major snapped at his son.

The Corporal stopped talking. He sat back into his chair and pondered the linoleum floor.

The Major recovered his composure to some extent. "What do you mean, 'she did'?" he demanded of his wife.

"She confessed to her husband," Violet said. "I heard her."

"She confessed?"

"She felt guilty," Violet continued. "She thought he was on his deathbed, so she confessed."

The Major looked over at Arlene. She was still wailing; nodding in agreement.

"She said you seduced her."

"Uncle William," Billie Jo said, "how could you?"

"Jesus!" The Major muttered.

"You just wait 'til Jesus and Abner Whitcomb get finished with you," Violet said.

"What's Abner Whitcomb got to do with this?"

"He's my lawyer," Violet said. "We're suing you for divorce." She walked over, sat next to The Corporal, and wrapped her arms around him. "And, Billy is going to live with me."

The Major was about to answer when Pamela Parkinson walked into the room. "Major," she said, "The Colonel wants to talk to you."

The Major's jaw dropped. "He's alive?" he said.

"We knew that an hour ago," Violet snapped.

"Thank Jesus!" the nurse said. "The bullet just creased his skull. He was unconscious for a few hours, but he's awake now."

"He's going to be okay?"

"We're still going to airlift him down to Little Rock for X-rays, but I think he'll recover nicely."

"No thanks to you," Arlene blurted out between wails.

"I didn't shoot him," The Major protested.

"You told 'im about me and that Jackie Moss," Billie Jo shouted. "That's why he went down there."

She turned to Arlene and the tears began to flow again. "I'm sorry, Mama, but nothing happened. I swear."

Arlene hugged her daughter.

The Major wanted to tell the truth. He wanted to say that he didn't tell anybody anything, but he knew that nobody there would listen. He decided to retreat, albeit briefly, from "enemy territory." He followed Pamela Parkinson down the hall to the first bedroom, opened the door and stepped inside. The nurse waited in the hallway.

There were two hospital beds, two straight-backed chairs, two bedside tables and one portable black-and-white television set in the room. Prints of Leonardo da Vinci's *The Last Supper* and Cassilly Adams' *Custer's Last Fight* adorned the walls.

Only one of the beds was occupied, and that was by The Colonel. He was wearing a hospital gown, and the left side of his forehead bore a large gauze bandage with spots of blood on it.

"Took your time getting here," The Colonel said.

"How are you, Frank?"

"I got shot in the head. How do think I am?"

"I didn't want that to happen."

"Babin's *your* friend."

"He's not my 'friend'. We were negotiating a business deal."

The Colonel scooted around; sat on the edge of the bed. "Well, that deal's never going to take place," he said. "We're talking about military secrets here, and we're not going to betray our country to that Czech Commie son-of-a-bitch."

"I told him that."

"Yeah?" the Colonel said. "Was that before or after you screwed my wife?"

The Major didn't answer his brother. He turned away and stared at the da Vinci print without actually seeing it.

"You think you're the only one?" The Colonel said. "Why do you think she drives down to Little Rock so often? She's got a guy there, too."

"Does she know that you know?'

"Of course not."

"Why do you tolerate it?" The Major asked.

"It keeps her out of my hair, or whatever's left of it," The Colonel said. "Most of the time, my wife can be a pain in the butt. It's much more peaceful here when she's down in Little Rock."

"I'm sorry, Frank," The Major said. "Things just got out of hand."

"We can talk about that later," The Colonel said. "Now, what's with Babin? And, what's this I hear about my daughter screwing that comedian?"

"I don't know if she was screwing him or not," The Major said. "She says she wasn't, but I saw her at the hotel."

"And…?"

"Babin concocted the story to cover what really happened. We told people that you heard about Billie Jo and the comedian. You came down to the hotel to confront him, and he shot you."

"And, they bought that?"

"There were no other witnesses. Just Babin and me."

"I can't believe this," The Colonel said. He lay back down onto the bed. "Do you really think this Moss fellow is going to go along with that lie? He's a famous man. When he starts talking to the press...."

"That's not going happen."

"What do you mean, 'it's not going to happen'?"

"Moss and his friend are not getting off the mountain. Babin is handling it."

The Colonel looked at his brother aghast. "Murder?" he said.

"An 'accident'."

"Are you insane?" The Colonel shouted. "We're not gangsters, here."

"What do you want, Frank?" The Major shouted back. "You want the military to come in and take over The Factory? You want us to go to prison?"

"The only one who's going to prison here is you," The Colonel said. "You've got to stop this thing."

"I don't know where they are," The Major said. "And, even if I did, it's already too late."

"Oh, shit!" The Colonel said, holding his head.

The door opened. Nurse Parkinson stepped into the room. "Are you all right, Colonel?" she asked her patient.

"My head is killing me."

She turned to The Major. "You can't upset him like this," she said. "He's had a major trauma."

"Give me something for the pain."

"I'll get some more aspirin," she said. "The helicopter should be here soon."

She turned to The Major. "Please wait outside," she said.

The Major walked out of the room, through the waiting area, which was still "enemy territory," and stepped outside. He lit a cigarette and began strolling the grounds of The Factory.

He knew he could reason with his brother, once he'd recovered from his injury and calmed down. At least, he hoped he could reason with him.

The Major circled the main building twice, then went upstairs to his office.

He was exhausted. He hadn't slept in well over twenty-four hours. He sat down behind his desk, retrieved the bottle of Johnny Walker and a glass from out of the bottom drawer and poured himself a drink. He leaned back and put his feet up on the open drawer.

The next thing he knew, according to the clock on his desk, it was three hours later. It had been the sound of the helicopter overhead that had awakened him.

The Major rubbed the sleep out of his eyes. He figured that the chopper was here to transport his brother to the hospital in Little Rock.

He started to stand up, and then he saw Edward at his office door. There were two Marines in utility uniforms behind him. They were carrying what looked like M16 rifles.

"Edward," he said, rising to his feet. "What are you doing here? What's going on?"

"William Dawson," Edward said, stepping forward and flashing his military credentials, "I'm here to arrest you."

"Arrest me?"

"The charge is treason and attempted murder."

17   CHAPTER SEVENTEEN

It was over.

At least, it was almost over.

I'm not sure if it was the F.B.I. or the Navy Department or whoever, but some branch of the Federal Government had Jackie and me stashed in connecting rooms at the luxurious, legendary Legacy Hotel in Little Rock. Even better (or worse), there were two armed Marine guards outside of our rooms.

How did we get there?

You'll recall that we had been up in the mountains, pretty much lost and trapped at the ranch of farmer Cody, the marijuana "kingpin." Jackie had got hold of Cody's shotgun. The two Olson behemoths were pointing their rifles at us. Cody's meshugge horse was blocking our retreat. And, the only thing that was preventing the next gunfight at the O.K. Corral was the fact that we were holding Cody between us and the Olsons.

Then, the "cavalry" had arrived.

They weren't on horses. No bugler was blowing the "Charge."

Actually, they arrived in a large military helicopter.

The sound of the whirling rotor blades may have been deafening, but the sight was beautiful, particularly when those half-dozen armed Marines lowered the ropes and began fast-lining down out of the aircraft.

The Olson brothers dropped their rifles and raised their hands.

Cody just stood there, his eyes wide with shock.

Jackie put down the shotgun.

The horse turned-tail, and ran back behind the barn.

And, the curious black bear was long gone.

While two of his men took charge of the weapons, a young first lieutenant walked up to Jackie and me. "Are you Jackie Moss?" he asked.

Jackie just nodded.

"I thought so," the Marine said. "I've seen you on the TV."

"Would you like an autograph?" Jackie said, a bit feebly.

The lieutenant turned to me. "You must be Mr. Arthur."

I felt like hugging the guy, but I only managed to say, "I'll give you an autograph, too."

"We're here to take you home, sir."

What the hell! Jackie beat me to it. He reached over and gave the somewhat surprised and embarrassed lieutenant a giant bear hug.

"How did you find us?" I asked, as the lieutenant and one of his men were escorting us over to the chopper.

"We've got a couple of first-rate trackers looking for you. Agent Benedict showed us where you entered the woods, and…."

Jackie interrupted the officer. "Agent Benedict?" he said.

"Yes, sir," the lieutenant replied. "She's with the F.B.I."

"She's F.B.I.!?!" Jackie said.

"Yes, sir."

"I'll be damned," Jackie said.

I felt exactly the same way.

"The trackers were following your trail," the lieutenant continued, "when they heard gunfire. They radioed us the approximate location, and here we are."

"You guys deserve medals," Jackie said.

"Just doing our duty, sir."

"You may not be aware of it, but you've just broken up a big drug ring here."

The lieutenant appeared confused. "Sir?"

"Marijuana."

"Take a look in the barn," I said.

"You'll find the mother lode," Jackie added.

"Sir," the lieutenant said, "I was told that this operation had to do with foreign espionage."

"Now, you're getting two for the price of one," Jackie said.

"I guess my captain better inform the DEA."

"Good idea," Jackie said. "You'll go far, son."

A Marine medic checked Jackie and me out. He took our blood pressures; treated some minor scrapes and scratches.

We were strapped into the helicopter for our ride down the mountain. As we were about to lift off, we watched the Marines securing Cody and the Olson brothers for later transport.

We also saw the horse. It had trotted back out from behind the barn, and he was standing at the Hefty garbage bag that Cody had dropped, munching away on its contents.

"That's going to be one happy horse," Jackie quipped.

The chopper rose up into the air, and I noticed the black bear. It was patiently watching the horse from the tree line. None of the Marines on the ground seemed to be aware of the animal.

"I'll bet he's waiting for the leftovers," I said to Jackie.

Jackie chuckled. "Stoned," he said, "they will be the best of buddies."

Momentarily, I visualized the horse and the bear frolicking together in the ranch yard.

It took only a few minutes for the helicopter to transport us down to the mountain road turn-out where we'd abandoned the smashed up Camaro.

There were another half-dozen Marines stationed around the cordoned-off area. Babin's BMW, minus Babin, and the Olson's pick-up were still there. A tow truck driver was in the process of hooking up the Camero, and a beige Chrysler Town & Country Station Wagon was parked a few yards up the road.

A tall weathered-looking gentleman in a gray suit, who could have passed as a stand-in for John Wayne, approached us as we got off the chopper. "Gentlemen," he said, "I'm Agent Cabot. Would you come with me, please?"

He motioned to the Town & Country, and the vehicle pulled forward.

"Where are we going?" I asked.

"Little Rock," Agent Cabot said. "For a debriefing."

I looked around. Jackie looked around. "Is Agent Benedict here?" he asked.

"No," Cabot said. "She's working elsewhere."

"We'd like to see her," Jackie said. "Thank her."

"I'll see what I can do." He motioned us to get into the back of the Town & Country.

I pointed to the two suitcases that Jackie and I had dropped when we'd headed for the hills. They were still where we'd left them. "Those are our suitcases over there," I said.

"Certainly," Agent Cabot said. He called to one of the Marines, who retrieved our luggage and stowed it into the back of the station wagon. Cabot got into the front passenger seat and the driver, who I assume was also a F.B.I. agent, drove us down the mountain.

"We'd really like to see Agent Benedict," Jackie said again.

"I'll see what I can do," Agent Cabot repeated.

And, that was the extent of our conversation with Agent Cabot down the mountain.

Jackie and I looked at each other, but both of us figured that it was probably best to keep quiet, since neither of us really knew what this "debriefing" was going to entail.

I guess we were already checked into the hotel, because Cabot and the other agent brought us up through the rear entrance to our rooms. We were allowed to shower, change clothes, order a meal via room service, and then told to wait.

I wanted to call my wife, to let her know that we were okay, but the hotel operator informed me that no outside lines were available.

Were we being held incommunicado?

I opened the door to my room and came face-to-face with a freckle-faced Marine corporal. "Yes, sir?" he said.

"I want to make a phone call," I said.

"That's not possible, sir."

"I want to call my wife. She hasn't heard for me in two days and she worries"

"I'm sorry, sir. I have my orders."

"Can I speak to Agent Cabot."

"He's not here now, sir."

"Then, I'd like to talk to your superior officer."

"He's not here either, sir," the corporal said. "Please step back inside the room."

"Are we prisoners here?"

"Please step back inside the room, sir," the corporal repeated. He rested his hand on his sidearm.

I retreated back into the room and looked at Jackie, who had been monitoring my exchange with our Marine keeper.

"Well, at least we've got room service," he said.

I lay down on my bed and, almost immediately, fell asleep.

Jackie lay down in his room and, almost immediately, fell asleep.

The next morning, we were having breakfast when there was a knock on the door. Without waiting for a response, Agent Cabot entered, followed by another suit, this one in his fifties, with salt-and-pepper hair, and a somewhat younger man with a shaved head in the uniform of a Navy commander.

"Good morning," Cabot said. No cheery smile.

"So, when are we getting out of here?" Jackie asked.

"Soon," Cabot said.

"How soon is soon?"

The salt-and-pepper suit stepped forward. "We have you booked back to Los Angeles on a two o'clock flight."

Cabot introduced the suit as F.B.I. Agent Spencer Bartholomew, who headed the Bureau's Public Relations wing in Washington, and his companion as his Navy counterpart, Commander Michael Griffin.

Jackie took a sip of his coffee. "I already have a publicist," he said.

"Could somebody please tell us what is going on here?" I said, trying to defuse the situation.

"I'd be glad to," Bartholomew said, flashing a grin. He grabbed the desk chair in the room and pulled it over to the table where Jackie and I were eating. Griffin and Cabot remained standing.

"We're going to take you into our confidence, gentlemen," Bartholomew said. "We've checked you out, and we know you're good Americans who wouldn't do anything to hurt your country."

"Of course not," Jackie and I said in unison.

I glanced at Jackie. He glanced at me. We both knew this guy was bullshitting us, but we were going to go along with him. Anything to get out of there.

"It seems," Bartholomew said, "that the two of you have accidentally stumbled across a plot to steal U.S. military secrets."

"We kinda figured that," Jackie said. "Was this Babin fella trying to steal the doo-hickey?"

Bartholomew appeared confused. "The 'doo-hickey'?"

"The gizmo for the Navy's missile program."

"That's right," Bartholomew said with a slight chuckle. "The 'doo-hickey'. I've never heard it referred to that way."

"That threat has now been neutralized," Griffin interjected.

"That is correct," Bartholomew added. "Mr. Babin and his co-conspirators are in custody."

"The Major?" I asked.

"Since the case is still under investigation, I'm not at liberty to discuss it in any further detail."

"Then, what do you need us for?" I asked. "Mr. Moss and I don't have any *direct* knowledge of Babin or anybody else stealing military secrets. We just put two and two together."

"And, it equaled four," Jackie said.

"I understand that," Bartholomew said.

"Everything else," I said, "like shooting The Colonel, was a frame-up."

"We know that," Bartholomew assured us, "and that's all gone away."

"Thank God," Jackie said.

"We're really here to ask you a favor," Bartholomew said.

"Oh! Oh!" Jackie said. "Here it comes."

"Listen to the man!" Cabot ordered.

Bartholomew threw the agent a stony glance, which shut him up. He turned back to us, and smiled again. "Believe me," he said. "You'll like this favor."

"What is it?" I asked.

"A few years ago, our government placed two undercover operatives in the town of Buford to keep an eye on our military interests; to prevent people like Mr. Babin from stealing them."

"And, one of them is Angie Benedict," Jackie said.

"That's correct," Bartholomew said. "How did you know that?"

"We just figured it out," Jackie said, not wanting to get the Marine lieutenant who'd rescued us into trouble.

"Who's the other one?" I asked.

"Edward Webster."

"The chauffeur?" Jackie said.

Bartholomew nodded. "He works for Navy Intelligence."

"I'll be damned," Jackie said, turning to me. "Did you figure that?" he asked.

"No idea," I said.

"And, we'd like to keep it that way," Bartholomew said. "Ms. Benedict and Mr. Webster are top operatives in our country's battle against crime and foreign countries bent on stealing our military secrets. They work undercover, and if their photographs or other information ever appeared in the press, not only would they lose their value, but also, possibly, their lives."

"We wouldn't want that to happen," Jackie said. "I like her. Him, too."

"How can we help?" I asked.

"The press has already picked up on our raid yesterday in Buford," Bartholomew said, "but they don't know what *really* happened. And, that's how you can help us."

"I don't understand." I said.

"We want you to hold a press conference."

"A press conference?" Jackie said.

"That's right," Bartholomew said. "You're already a famous person, Mr. Moss. And now, you're going to be a national hero."

Jackie pondered that idea for a moment. "A national hero?" he said. "I like that idea."

CHAPTER EIGHTEEN

The tall tale that Agent Bartholomew and Commander Griffin concocted for us to relate to the press was a beaut, inspired by *The Thirty-Nine Steps*, *The Man Who Knew Too Much* or some other Alfred Hitchcock thriller. After all, Hitchcock had his "MacGuffin," and we had our "doo-hickey."

With the two "authors" standing beside us, Jackie and I conveyed our story at a press conference in a meeting room in the Legacy Hotel. There were, probably, a half dozen reporters there, two or three photographers and a couple of television cameramen.

Our fiction went something like this: Jackie and I were in Buford, performing at The General's birthday gig, when we overheard a conversation that led us to believe that some people at the affair were plotting to steal government secrets. Because they were hidden behind a partition, neither of us could see the persons who were discussing these nefarious plans, but we agreed that the authorities should be called, and the moment we got back to the hotel, we'd phoned the F.B.I.

Next morning, on our way down the mountain to catch our plane at the Little Rock Airport, our car had had a flat. In seeking help, we'd stumbled across the largest marijuana growing operation in the state of Arkansas and, soon after that, the Marines, swooped in and rescued us.

Eat your heart out, Alfred Hitchcock.

Neither Angie Benedict's nor Edward Webster's names ever entered our narrative.

Frankly, I didn't buy the story. Jackie didn't buy the story. I don't think the press bought the story, but if you want to believe it, I've got that bridge in Brooklyn I can sell you cheap.

The reporters started throwing specific questions at us, but before we could answer most of them, Agent Bartholomew stepped in and said, "That's classified information."

After about twenty minutes of this back-and-forth, Bartholomew announced: "You must remember, ladies and gentleman, that Mr. Moss and Mr. Arthur are heroes. They risked their lives to protect our nation's military secrets, and they also brought down a dangerous drug dealer."

Jackie and I tried our best to appear humble and not giggle. But, I almost lost it when Jackie leaned over and whispered to me, "Dangerous? Gee, I was more afraid of the horse."

After the press conference, Bartholomew and Griffin drove us to the airport.

"Any chance I could see Angie Benedict before we go?" Jackie asked, as we watched the city of Little Rock whisk by. "I'd like to thank her."

"I'm afraid she's already left the state," Bartholomew said. "I'm sure she knows you're grateful."

"Could you give her a message for me?"

"If I can."

"Ask her, if she ever gets to Los Angeles, to call me. I'd like to take her to lunch or dinner."

"I'll see what I can do." Bartholomew said, but from the tone of his voice, both Jackie and I knew that he'd do nothing.

The two government press representatives took us directly to our plane. Griffin handed us our tickets, thanked us and told us that we'd be met by agents at LAX.

Back in Los Angeles, in order to avoid the press, we were deplaned through the back door of the aircraft by two F.B.I. agents and driven to our homes.

Jackie was dropped off first in Beverly Hills. "I'll call you tomorrow," he said, as he headed for his front door.

"Wait 'til the end of the week," I said. "I need a few days off."

He gave me a "thumbs up," then entered the single story house, as our car headed out of his driveway on its way to my home in the San Fernando Valley.

Next morning, I was pissed when my wife, Doris, woke me out of a deep sleep around eleven. "What?" I said, then regretted that I'd snapped at her.

She handed me the morning newspaper. Jackie's and my photo were on the top half of the front page, below a headline that read: "COMIC MOSS BRINGS DOWN ESPIONAGE RING."

I sat in bed for a minute, staring at the article, without really reading it.

"Jackie's on the phone," she said. She re-connected the jack to the bedside phone that I had disconnected the night before. "He insists on talking to you."

"What, Jackie?" I snapped into the receiver.

"Have you seen the paper?" he asked.

"I'm looking at it now. It's bullshit!"

"I know," Jackie said, "but it's terrific bullshit. Ray Crystal called first thing this morning. They want me back at the Jackpot, but he's also had calls from the Sahara and the Riviera."

"That's great," I said.

"He's even had inquiries from clubs in New York and Miami."

"When you're hot, you're hot," I said.

And, Jackie *was* "hot" again.

Over the next couple of years, we played major clubs in New York, Chicago, Miami and, of course, Las Vegas.

Jackie mellowed. He was still as funny as he ever was, but after our experience in Buford, his innate anger seemed to disappear. He became more pliable, and didn't take offense at every little thing. The truth was, as we both knew, we were lucky to be alive.

Jackie even wound up doing a hit television series, *Bachelor Digs*.

He wasn't the star. The leads in this somewhat progressive show were a couple of young guys, one white, one black, who rent a two-bedroom apartment together. Jackie played the landlord who'd drop in once or twice during each half-hour episode, get his laughs, and then depart.

The series ran for six years and, while Jackie was doing that, I was home writing music. I even wrote the theme song for the series, which earned me a nice check every time the show aired in first or reruns.

So, life was, and is, good.

I know you're wondering what happened to Angie Benedict, Paul Babin, the Dawson family up in Buford and everybody else.

One night, a year or so after Buford, Angie Benedict showed up at the club date Jackie and I were playing in Chicago. She was no longer working undercover. In fact, she'd left the F.B.I., and was now the head of security for some big national corporation.

Who could blame her? What kind of life can a person have if they're always undercover?

We were both delighted to see here. We spent almost two hours catching up after the show, and then she and Jackie went off together to talk.

I hate to disappoint you, but the violins didn't play. The great romance you were hoping for didn't happen.

Jackie and Angie Benedict spent about an hour chatting. They hugged each other, and then she went off by herself. As far as I know, they've never seen each other since.

Jackie wasn't heartbroken. Back in Los Angeles, he'd become involved with Judy Dobrin, an independent casting director. They married a few months later, and they're still together.

Even better, Barbara, Jackie's ex, also remarried and now, twice a year, she sends Jason to Los Angeles to spend time with his father.

Angie Benedict (or Goodwin, or whatever her real name was) did, however, without violating national security, give us a short postscript as to what had happened in Buford after we'd left.

Paul Babin recovered from his wound and, as Angie had predicted, was eventually traded for one of "our guys" that was being held by "the other side."

Cody and the Olson brothers were turned over to the DEA, and they were "prosecuted to the full extent of the law"… whatever that was.

I have no idea what happened to Cody's meshugge horse, but I'm sure it found a home somewhere.

As for the black bear?

I don't know. Maybe he found Cody's marijuana field and is having a blast.

Edward Webster received a promotion, and is now supervising other undercover agents for Navy Intelligence.

And, the Dawsons?

They made a deal with the Federal Government. Since no government secrets had actually fallen into enemy hands, in exchange for dropping all charges against The Major, The Colonel agreed to sign over all rights to the "doo-hickey" to the Department of the Navy.

Violet didn't divorce The Major. The Colonel didn't divorce Arlene.

The Major, however, was demoted to Second Lieutenant.

Family, after all, is family.

Now, Buford is back to just manufacturing toilet seats.

But, they are marvelous toilet seats.

As many great men in history have said: "Fame is fleeting." Jake Moss, the country-western singer who was so "hot" back in the day....

What ever happened to him?

ABOUT THE AUTHOR

Michael B. Druxman is a veteran Hollywood screenwriter whose credits include *Cheyenne Warrior* with Kelly Preston; *Dillinger and Capone* starring Martin Sheen and F. Murray Abraham; and *The Doorway* with Roy Scheider, which he also directed.

He is also a prolific playwright, his one-person play, *Jolson*, having had numerous productions around the country. Other produced stage credits include one-person plays about Clark Gable, Carole Lombard, Spencer Tracy and Orson Welles. These and plays about Errol Flynn, Maurice Chevalier, Clara Bow, Basil Rathbone and Jeanette MacDonald and Nelson Eddy, as well as *B Movie*, a three-character play that deals with the sordid 1950s sex scandal involving actors Franchot Tone, Barbara Payton and Tom Neal, *Sexy Rexy*, a five character play about Rex Harrison and the women in his life, and *Lana & Johnny Were Lovers*, a four character play about the Lana Turner/Johnny Stompanato affair, have been individually published under the collective title of *The Hollywood Legends*.

His most recent contributions to *The Hollywood Legends* collection are *Robinson & Raft*, a three-character play dealing with movie tough guys Edward G. Robinson and George Raft, *The Last Monsters*, a five-character play featuring horror icons Lon Chaney, Jr., Bela Lugosi and John Carradine, and *Ava & Her Guys*, focusing on Ava Gardner and husbands Mickey Rooney, Artie Shaw and Frank Sinatra.

Additionally, Mr. Druxman is the author of more than fifteen published books, including several nonfiction works about Hollywood, its movies, and the people who make them (e.g., *Paul Muni: His Life and His Films*, *Basil Rathbone: His Life and His Films*, *Make It Again, Sam: A Survey of Movie Remakes*, *One Good Film De-*

serves Another: A Survey of Movie Sequels, Charlton Heston, Merv [Griffin], *The Musical: From Broadway to Hollywood, Miss Dinah Shore,* and *Hollywood Snapshots: The Forgotten Interviews*.

He has written three novels, *Nobody Drowns in Mineral Lake, Shadow Watcher* and *Murder in Babylon,* a book of short stories, entitled *Dracula Meets Jack the Ripper & Other Revisionist Histories,* plus the humorous revisionist history, *Once Upon a Time in Hollywood: From the Secret Files of Harry Pennypacker,* and *Family Secret,* a non-fiction book co-authored with Warren Hull, which reveals the true facts behind the 1947 murder of mobster "Bugsy" Siegel in Beverly Hills.

An acknowledged Hollywood historian, he has also written television documentaries and has been interviewed for various retrospective featurettes that have accompanied DVD releases of classic films (e.g. *The Maltese Falcon, The Hound of the Baskervilles,* etc.).

Mr. Druxman is a former Hollywood publicist of 35 years' experience who has represented many film and television stars, as well as noted directors, producers and composers. One of his Academy Award campaigns is often mentioned in books dealing with Oscar's history.

He has taught various dramatic writing and film appreciation courses in an adult university and is the author of *How to Write a Story…Any Story: The Art of Storytelling,* which has been used as a text in several colleges. He is often invited to speak to groups of aspiring film and television professionals to discuss screenwriting and the realities of show business.

A native of Seattle who graduated from Garfield High School and the University of Washington, Mr. Druxman moved with his wife, Sandy, from Los Angeles to Austin, TX in 2009.

His memoirs, *My Forty-Five Years in Hollywood and How I Escaped Alive* (2010) and *Life, Liberty & The Pursuit of Hollywood* (2013) are published by Bear Manor Media.

www.ingramcontent.com/pod-product-compliance
Lightning Source LLC
Chambersburg PA
CBHW071126250626
47159CB00006B/2146